The So
POUNCE

Homestead Harmonies

Nita G. Berquist

outskirtspress
DENVER, COLORADO

The Song of Pounce
Homestead Harmonies
All Rights Reserved.
Copyright © 2012 Nita G. Berquist
v3.0

Photos by: Fran Bryant, owner of Francor Photography in Kent, Washington

Outskirts Press, Inc.
http://www.outskirtspress.com

ISBN: 978-1-4327-8346-4

Outskirts Press and the "OP" logo are trademarks belonging to Outskirts Press, Inc.

PRINTED IN THE UNITED STATES OF AMERICA

About the Author

Nita Berquist has been a Bible teacher for over forty years and currently lives and writes in Kent, Washington. Her Biblical studies, *The Greatest Physician, Studies On healing; Somewhere With God, Studies On Being Led By His Spirit;* and *Smokescreens, Studies On Truth And Counterfeits* are also available for order through all booksellers. These studies are fiinding acceptance in a number of other countries as well as in the USA.

Nita's cats are Spackle, a young spotted male cat whose picture is on the cover of this book, his spotted brother Speckle, an orange girl cat with orange eyes named Jumper, and Spacer, a mature tabby female who has Bengal spots on her belly and classic sliver swirls on her sides. These cats were adopted from local animal shelters and they approved this book only after being told that they could have a small role in the next Pounce story.

You may follow Nita's writing and work on popular social networks or you may contact her by writing PO Box 5458, or PO Box 5339, Kent, WA 98064. Follow Pounce's adventures and tales of other people and animals in upcoming stories for young people and their grown-ups.

The Song Of Pounce is Nita's first book for youngsters and oldsters alike and has been granny and kid tested. They are waiting for Pounce's second book and his new adventures. Watch for it!

Thanks

Special thanks goes to Justin Lance, the general manager at Bahama Breeze Restaurant in Tukwilla, Washington. I've eaten hundreds of tasty shrimp while editing this story as I sit and listen to Caribbean music and think warmer thoughts of warmer places while our winter rains hit the windows. Thanks, Justin, and thanks also to Doug and the others who have served me with so much humor and patience.

Gaile Watkins and Maggy Angell have poured so many glasses of ice tea that I'm nearly afloat. They work at the Red Robin Restaurant in Covengton, Washington, and we've shared lots of pussycat tales and photos as I've edited this story while tucked up in a booth. Thanks, ladies.

Shane DeLaCruz, at the Red Robin Restaurant in Kent, Washington, has also waited on me and watched over my editing in the afternoons under their sunroom windows. I've no idea how many Teriyaki burgers I've eaten in that cozy spot but even Pounce would approve. Thanks, Shane.

By now you must think I eat out a lot. Well, I've found that writing in my office is a quiet occupation and rightly so, but editing, for me, requires the noise that living beings make. I have often found a new wrinkle for a story while watching and listening to people interact. I tried the library but it was too quiet. A mid-afternoon meal, with just enough activity and endless iced tea, has made this cat lady a happy camper during the editing process.

More thanks go to Donna Duncan, Anna Gregory, Floyde and Sharon Woods, Shirley Bayless, and my beloved David and Kristin and family. You all admire courage in others even when found in a fictional cat story. Some of you have read for me and all of you have listened to my ramblings. What would I have done without your ears? You folks have helped me herd my cats on paper from chapter to chapter, which was a difficult assignment, and all the while I rattled on about the real cats at home. What a blessing you are to me.

My son David, you listen and listen when I talk and you must love your Mom for you're never impatient when I chatter on and on. And Kristin, thank you for your suggestions and the time you've taken to read for me. I can feel your prayers. Family is dearer with each passing year.

A special thanks goes to you, Sarah Wimmer. We send countless chapters and ideas back and forth and you are the lady who checks everything I write. Your hard work, common good sense, and willingness to research gives you an edge, especially over me for I think in odd bunny-hole directions and you help me keep ideas connected. Your red pencil makes my life miserable before making my life deliciously happy. I dislike you when you discomfort me and love you again when you comfort me. How childish is that?

Well, now we've done it again and God has helped us finish another book. But look, Pounce and his friends are roaming the pages of his second book these days, and I plan to discomfort you, upset you, and torment you with useless commas and lots of prepositions hanging here and there. Sarah? Sarah? Don't go away. Ah, there you are.

Thanks again, everyone, and now let's trust that countless readers of every age will enjoy Pounce's story.

_____Nita G Berquist

Dedication

This story is first of all for Pounce but, since he never learned to read, it is also for all the young humans who pounce into the world, take a look around, and love life anyway. I dedicate this story to all those people and critters who, in courageous knowing or in bold ignorance, pounce on living and enjoy the journey. And especially I dedicate this story to Dillon, a little boy, who at four doesn't know yet what to pounce on but is determined to pounce on all of life anyway.

Once, when I needed him, the real Pounce cat came along. He chose me at my local animal shelter after we had studied each other in a private room for many minutes. I did not call him, touch him, or pet him. I just watched him. He watched back. I wondered why he was so quiet and uninterested in coming to me.

The agent returned and asked if I'd take him. "He's been here a number of months and been sick too. Will you take him away for twenty dollars?"

The going rate was fifty dollars and I wondered what she wasn't telling me. Then Pounce made the first move, a trait he kept up for the next couple of years. He stretched out his paw from the chair where he sat next to my chair, placed it on my arm, and stared intently into my face. He didn't extend his claws but I could feel them just barely pricking me. You might say he touched me for a twenty.

"I guess that's a yes," I replied. That twenty was the first of a dozen or so. The vet got the others.

Pounce had short, spotted, black and white hair; long, powerful hind legs; and a silly look on his mottled face. He was young, not a kitten but not yet an adult. I guess he was a teen cat. He taught me to laugh when I found laughing hard. His bright, empty eyes and funny little ways reminded me not to evaluate him by what I saw for he had plenty inside that spotted hide of his.

I quickly learned to watch him closely. He played fetch and brought back whatever I threw for him. Then at dinner I started carrying everything at once on a tray since, if I didn't, he would drink tea out of my cup and swipe food off my plate before I could get the entire meal onto the table.

I tried locking him up but Pounce opened doors. Sliding doors and doors with knobs were no challenge to this cat. So I decided to tie him up. I put him in a cat harness, then in a dog harness attached to a collar and leash, and finally into two harnesses and a collar. He came out of all of them in seconds, no matter how tightly I buckled him in. On my last try he put his open jaw through one strap and twisted his body around. I thought his jaw was broken and cut him out of the harness with a knife while he lay twisted upside down in my lap. I told him that we could get rich if he would train as a movie cat, but he wasn't interested in film, just in staying out of constraints of any kind.

Pounce curled around the top of my head at night and pulled soft curlers out of my hair. I started curling my hair in the morning. I was the grandmother, lying in her bed wearing her hairy night stocking cap, neatly secured under the chin by a long black tail. Pounce got me up in the morning by breathing heavily in my ear. If that didn't work, if I ignored him, he bit my ear just hard enough to make sure I was listening. I got up.

We watched television with him sitting on top of my head for the best view. When he grew to over five pounds, he lay around my shoulders, a point I insisted upon. His favorite shows were the Madison Square Garden dog show, any PBS special on cats, local horse racing, and an occasional football game. We took walks together. Well, I walked and he rode on my shoulder, swishing his tail and swinging his head to see everything. When he reached eleven pounds, I stopped walking. Watching horse racing must have given him the idea of handicapping me.

Pounce would watch the words appear on the computer screen as I wrote this book, but he preferred to walk on the keyboard and write it himself. I was pretty sure he couldn't read and found out for sure when I checked his spelling. I read my rough draft to him and he was a good listener until he didn't like something. Then he pushed against my face and demanded that I stop reading. If I didn't, he plopped down on the pages and began chewing holes in the ones he thought needed help. He would push his front paws together until the paper buckled in the middle and then he'd chew a large hole in the center. I told him the best words were in the middle but he didn't care. I did a lot of rewriting around his chewing face, big rear end, and swishing tail.

Did I mention that he liked honey in his tea? To enjoy my own cup, I finally gave in and made a cup for him too. Granny and Pounce would often sit on the porch enjoying their evening tea together. There's something vastly entertaining about watching a cat with his head buried in a teacup; his long white whiskers plastered back, sticking out on both sides of the cup, twitching in rhythm to his lapping.

He studied my drawings, played the piano with me, slept on my head, and stole every little thing I forgot to button up or nail down, including my heart. I laughed, I chortled, and I hooted for several years until this lovely, empty-headed feline was gone. Though Pounce is now only an achingly pleasant, warm memory, I've gone on laughing and pouncing.

Ah, Pounce. This is for you.

Contents

1

Welcome Wounded

"How did that get in? Is that another cat?" The deep voice shook the room with demanding authority. The sound swirled around the terrified cat's ears as he squatted, blinking and shaking and pressing his little body hard against the kitchen baseboard cabinet. A man as large as his sound stepped through the door into the yellow light of the kitchen and stomped his big feet on the rug by the door as he spoke.

A softer, lighter voice quieted his booming. "Hush, Matthew. You're too loud. He can hear mice, you know. Of course it's a cat. I found him hunched by the barn; under the old double plow he was, all scrunched up and wet, poor thing, held there by Wally."

At the sound of his name, the old dog that had followed the man inside stood up from the rug by the kitchen door and waved his tail slowly. His regal bearing and his coat, though matted and wet, revealed the fine heritage of the big, gold and white collie.

"Ah, Wall. It's enough. Rest now." Matthew coughed as he spoke. The cold, wet rain had chilled the big man and he shivered as he slipped out of his dripping raincoat and hung it by the door. Wally turned and settled once more on the now muddy rag rug, letting out a great sigh as he dropped again.

Pounce continued to shake. He felt sick and too exhausted to run again, but there was still a little fight left in him if needed so he kept his eyes focused on the dog at the door. He breathed in shallow puffs, the light hurt his eyes, his torn paws stung, and he could not remember the last time he had tasted food. He pulled his matted tail tighter under his body and continued to squat, a trembling and shivering little bundle of wet and torn hair. It was hard to see what color he was under all that mud. Water dripped off his short coat and pooled on the floor.

"What a mess," Matthew growled as he stared at the cat while reaching across the counter for the coffee pot. He poured half a cup and lifted it to his mouth as his wife addressed him.

"Help me, dear. Use this to pick him up and place him on the table." Bonny pushed a big towel at Matthew and he sighed as he put his untouched coffee cup back on the countertop.

"Oh, poor kitty. See how thin he is. Oh, kitty, kitty." This higher pitched voice sounded soft to Pounce and he liked the tone but, before he could think about it, the big man suddenly draped a towel over him and pushed it under his body. Holding him tightly, Matthew easily felt his ribs through the towel. The tense and shaking cat couldn't breathe deeply and his side hurt, but he didn't struggle as Matthew's hands lifted him gently above the wooden table before setting the towel bundle in the middle of it.

My empty stomach, Pounce groaned, making a tiny cat sound, "Eeew."

Bonny did not miss it. "Here, Matthew, you hold him still on the table while I see if he can still swallow." Turning to the stove, Bonny pulled a ladle half full of chicken broth up from the depths of a deep pot and carefully poured it into a shallow bowl. Into this she ran a bit of cool water from the sink faucet. Pounce felt his head being pushed down into the dish. His nose and mouth and chin and whiskers were covered with chicken broth. He struggled to stand and escape while licking his nose and mouth—licking that delicious broth! It was so delicious that he forgot the towel and strong hands that still held him.

Mama kitty, this is good. Pounce breathed his pleasure as he lowered his head into the dish and lapped the bowl clean. The humans seemed pleased.

After that, it didn't take long for Bonny's skilled fingers exploring the body of the cat to determine the extent of his injuries. She pulled the towel back a little at a time, rubbing some of the mud and dirt out of the hair as she did. She parted his spotted black and white coat and gently probed through the dirty hair and torn skin.

"Oh, poor kitty. How did this happen to you? Poor kitty." This murmuring was accompanied by soft clucking noises Bonny made with her tongue, all of which reassured and comforted Pounce. His terrible fear when chased through the barbed wire fence by the coyote, followed by his total panic when cornered by the big collie, now gave way to calm, slow, rhythmic breathing. In that funny feline way that only cats know, his eyes closed and opened again slowly, making them appear to be half moon slits as his whiskers first twitched and then relaxed with the rest of his battered frame. The woman's diagnosis soon followed.

"He's got broken ribs, or maybe he's just bruised. Something hit him in his side."

A bicycle, Pounce thought to himself. *I didn't see it coming.*

Pulling the towel back further, the woman continued murmuring. "His footpads have deep cuts, no doubt from walking here. That's strange. Look at the way his pads are torn. They look sliced and bubbly too. Matthew, look!"

The big man started to bend low over the cat but Bonny bent even lower, blocking his view. "Matthew! What's this? Burnt hair? Why lots of places are burned. Look at his hind legs and his belly!" The little round woman seldom raised her voice, but this time her voice was loud enough to cause the collie to raise his head and look at her in concern. "This cat's been burned! Feel the cooked fur on his legs and belly. How could such a thing happen?"

Bonny fought back tears as Matthew thoughtfully ran a hand over Pounce's hind leg, pulling it straight as he did and studying the inside of it carefully. His eyes hardened as his fingers pressed open the charred hair though he said nothing.

Bonny sighed loudly. "Well, I don't think his skin is cooked, but his hair is burnt right up to his hide. Poor baby. I'll have to cut that wet stuff off. Burnt hair stinks. Ugh!" She wrinkled her nose at the smell but then went back to crooning over the cat an instant later. Nothing could stop Bonny once she was in rescue mode. Matthew sighed and prepared himself for however long it would take Bonny to "fix" the cat. His coffee would have to wait.

Pounce hung his head and stared down at the table. It was splashed with light from the overhead lamp and his own funny shadow moved as he swung his head from side to side. Under normal circumstances he would have been fascinated by the moving shadow, but nothing was normal now. Instead, he shook his head again and tried to push away the image of the jeering boys who had thrown him into the dump on the edge of town, that awful burning dump. It was a painful and terrifying memory.

"Honey, his head and ears are not burned and most of his whiskers seem to be here, except for a few curled ones, but how would a cat get burned? Wouldn't it run away?" Unbidden tears popped up in the woman's eyes as she studied her small charge.

"Now, dear, he'll be all right, you'll see. You'll see." Matthew brought one large hand out of the folds of the towel and squeezed his wife's shoulder.

Pounce swung his head toward the deep voice. *So the man could talk without roaring after all?* That too was comforting to the cat. Everything in his life lately had been noisy or painful. He put his head back down on the towel while Bonny continued her examination.

"This poor guy's been chased, no doubt through some barbed wire somewhere. His hide is ripped. See his hip? It's going to be apiece before he'll be catching mice again."

"Heh! If'n he ever!" Matthew's voice boomed around the kitchen, once again his normal, loud self.

"Now don't you go carrying on, Matthew. Dr. Lee should see this kitty and fix him up and he'll make a good barn cat. You'll see."

"We's got good barn cats," Matthew roared, making Pounce cower as low as he could in the towel and start trembling again. "And we'll do this cat just like the other one. We've got all the stuff right here in the kitchen."

"We *have* good barn cats," Bonny calmly corrected him and smiled fondly at her man. "And, stop shouting. See how you frighten the little thing?"

To the cat, it all became a blur then. The woman clipped off a great deal of his hair, from everywhere it seemed, and she was especially careful to clip where he was burned on his belly and legs and to check his skin for burns. There were a few raw places on his belly and hind legs where the heat had done more than burn hair, but not many.

Bonny wiped him down all over with a warm, wet cloth, making sure he was clean and then rubbed some stinking stuff into his wounds. Pounce pulled his head to the side to get away from the smell but Matthew held him firmly upside down while Bonny treated his legs and belly. She tore some thin, white fabric, put more stinky grease on his pads and bandaged his feet and lower legs. He looked like he was wearing large white shoes over his little white paws.

The rip in his hip was jagged and long and had to be carefully sewn to catch all the edges. Bonny used a very thin thread and a small needle for the job. Pounce was again wrapped tightly in the towel and held by Matthew with just his hip and tail exposed. Bonny first clipped all the hair away from the wound, dried it, and then dusted some kind of powder over it. Then she took hold of the flap of skin and began stitching it down.

"Well, this powder's still here in the kitchen since we sewed up Catcher, but I suppose you'll take it back down to the barn now. Right?"

"It's what the vet give me, woman," the loud grunt replied.

"What the vet *gave* me, Matthew," the soft voice corrected him again. "Though you know what Doctor Lee told you. You've got to throw out these old remedies and stop trying to use up everything that old Doc Reggie gave you. When we sewed up Catcher, Doctor Lee told you she should have had an antibiotic and something for pain too. Thank God, she never got an infection, but here we go again. This little cat should see a vet, and what is this powder anyway that we keep pouring into animal wounds? Is it still any good?"

"Yah, whatever, cats is tough." The grunt came back kindly without answering her directly. Matthew was not about to spend good money for a vet to fix a barn cat, or any other animal that he could take care of at home on the farm. *That's what those modern city folks do, but farm folks do their own vettin', at least the small stuff.* Matthew kept these thoughts to himself for this was old ground, and he was tired and wet and didn't feel like plowing up an old conversation again.

"Cats *are* tough, Matthew, and even so, sewing them up like this hurts. And that's that!" Bonny had lived with him long enough to know what he was thinking and, though he resisted change, she also knew that he would change in the end. He always did. So she kept sewing without saying anything else since Pounce was quiet and not fighting her. *The tug of the sewing in his skin isn't adding much more to the discomfort he already feels*, she thought.

Matthew had not released his firm grip around the towel and continued to hold the cat tightly. His hands were so large that it was an easy job, and only the quick swishing of the cat's tail let the people know that the kitty was uncomfortable.

As she sewed, Bonny spoke again. "Now about this cat—you

and I have been sewing and doctoring all of these years but things are different now and we've a good man and friend in Doctor Lee. Next time, we'll call him." Bonny kept smiling without looking up but her firm tone told Matthew that she was serious.

"Yah. Okay, honey. After this, if'n it needs sewin' up and such, we'll call the Doc." Matthew sighed and inwardly relaxed. He would yield after all. His beloved Bonny had the bit in her teeth about this issue, so it was over.

Pounce lay as still as he could. After Bonny put in the last stitch, he began to have an unreasonable desire to purr. He fought the desire for a few moments. But finally he yielded to the rumbling inside, and a sound as welcome as spring bees began buzzing through the room. Pounce continued to purr as the country couple bent over him and clipped and washed and powdered other places on his beat-up hide.

"Ay, Matthew. Listen to our kitty. He knows we're trying to help him."

"Haw! Your kitty!"

The growling man stuck one finger out from his massive hand, found an uninjured spot on Pounce's head and began to gently rub it. Bonny chuckled. Matthew petting the cat with one finger did not escape her keen eyes. By this time she had clipped most of the hair on Pounce's sides though she left a strip of black and white blotched hair running down the middle of his back. She did not find any rips or burns on his back or tail. Pounce felt grateful for every hair he had left on his frame.

"And what shall I call you, pussycat?" The woman purred at the cat as she powdered yet another small rip in his hide. Pounce could not tell her that his name was Pounce. But he kept saying his own name in his head, and finally he tried to purr and meow at the same time. After a number of tries it came out of his throat close to what it should be.

"Purr-ounce. Purr-ounce."

"Ah, I know. I'll call you Pounce. Things tried to pounce on you and here you are, pouncing right into our lives, you lovely kitty, you." Bonny crooned as she petted her rescued feline. Pounce purred his name even louder then and smiled with his eyes as tight and slit-like as he could. "Purr-ounce. Purr-ounce. Purr-ounce."

Matthew shook his head, groaned loudly and turned to go, leaving the cat and his wife purring to each other. "Cows. Someone's got chores, you know. I hope there's chicken soup on the table and not cat when I finish up."

At this Bonny chuckled again and nodded as Matthew put on his raincoat and cap and opened the kitchen door, his now cold coffee forgotten on the counter behind him.

"Hey, Wall. Cows." The old collie was on his feet in an instant and dashed across the yard toward the pasture as soon as the door spit him out. Ignoring the dog, Matthew slipped and splashed across the muddy yard to the barn where he paused to open the gate from the pasture into the milking room. Followed by Wally, three cows trailed after the big man into the building.

Bonny left Pounce purring and sprawled on the table. She pulled the deep middle drawer of an old dresser by the side of the fireplace out about halfway. Taking out heavy woolen socks and a few thin ones from it, she left with an armload of socks and returned carrying a thick towel that she placed in the drawer followed by Pounce himself.

"This is your bed, kitty, until you are working in the barn. You are up here above Wally though he would never hurt you. He didn't hurt you, did he?"

She spoke softly as she lowered Pounce onto his towel bed and gently rubbed his ears. Pounce had to admit to himself that it was true. He had been cornered but not harmed by the dog. Such an admission was humbling for he had believed that all dogs were cat killers when given the chance. Now, he was more than glad his belief had been wrong.

He was too tired to think any more. Though he hurt all over, almost at once Pounce sank into a deep sleep in his new bed. His slumber was not even shaken by the door slamming loudly behind Matthew and Wally when they returned from their chores in the barn.

Pounce thrashed in his dresser drawer bed during the early part of his sleep and Bonny kept watch until he grew quiet and was still. For several days and nights he didn't move much except to drink broth, nibble on small bits of chicken, and thrash a bit as he dreamed of being cold, frightened, in pain, and finally curled up somewhere warm. The curled up warm part was the best part of his dreams. Finally he realized that he actually was warm and his belly really was full and, for the present, that was enough. Pounce didn't think about anything else.

CHAPTER 2

Getting Acquainted

It was days before Pounce began to feel like his old self but, one morning, he awoke in his dresser bed and saw that he'd kicked several of his bandage boots off during the night. So he stretched and yawned and then began to pull off the other two boots with his teeth.

He stretched his toes on each foot and studied his footpads. *Yup, just like new,* he thought and, looking down at the floor, he sprang out and landed on the small rug in front of the dresser.

"Ouch! A little tender yet." Pounce grunted out loud, stretched again with his tail and butt stuck high into the air and kneaded the rug with his front claws. One last stretch, but this time he inverted his spine and stuck his hind legs out behind him one at a time.

"Ah, the kitty is back and all his parts seem to be working too." Pounce grinned at his own humor, smacked his lips, and listened to his growling stomach. "I wonder when she will feed me?" He meowed as he licked his lips again.

Each day Bonny had fed him wonderful things and his inner clock was striking the memory of early morning feedings. On this morning the country couple had left the house early. He didn't see the food but he could smell wonderful things in the kitchen and sniffed in appreciation again and decided that, until the woman fed him, he should explore his surroundings.

There were several large rugs in the room. One lay under the heavy kitchen table, and another lay in front of the alcove of windows that jutted out, overlooking the garden and the field beyond. Two easy chairs sat on it near the window that usually filled the house with light from the afternoon sun. A magazine holder sat by the large chair and a knitting satchel full of yarn by the smaller one. Pounce remembered yarn balls he had played with as a kitten and grinned with simple pleasure at the thought. *Yes. Balls of yarn to unroll.*

These two rugs were designed with flowers and scrolling leaves and were made of thick wool with rolled edges all the way around. They felt deep under the cat's pads. Pounce sniffed the wool on the rug in front of the window and then dropped and rolled back and forth several times, rubbing his spine on the rug. Standing, he looked down and focused on a large flower under his front feet. *Feet? You like?* He laughed. His habit of entertaining himself remained undiminished by his recent misfortunes.

Next, he stood on his hind legs and sniffed a beautiful, cushioned bench that nestled under the windows. Its back was made of a series of striped pillows and the bench itself was awash with colors of blue, green, and yellow, skillfully worked in wool. He studied the bench and cushions and had thoughts of hours of warm afternoon sunlight cooking his battered body. It made Pounce break into a typical Pounce song.

> "Catnaps are coming.
> I'm sleeping and sunning
> And dreaming of not running.
> My catnaps are coming again.
> Yeah."

He addressed his feet again, and once more kneaded the rug before walking across the hardwood floor to the rag rug that ran in front of the fireplace. It was made of old blankets and coats.

Two chairs rested on it, one on each end, plus a little stool on which he saw several strips of leather and a leather punch. He sniffed the leather and liked the smell.

Pounce looked up at the mantle over the fireplace. A picture of a young man in uniform sitting astride a bay horse was on one end. Two glass candlesticks were next to the frame and in the middle of the mantle was an American flag folded up inside a triangular wooden box. Morning light crossed the room from the kitchen window and sparkled and bounced off the candlesticks, creating miniature rainbows. A small chest of carved wood and a cherry glass bowl were on the other end of the mantel.

The cat wondered what was in them. *I'll leap up and look when my feet aren't so tender,* crossed his mind. He made his plan and then instantly, in cat fashion, forgot it as he turned his attention elsewhere. Small rag rugs were scattered throughout the entire room and half a dozen were draped over a sawhorse that sat near the front door. An unfinished rug and some coils of sewn-together wool strips lay half on and half off the rocking chair on the right side of the fireplace. Though the couple had numerous items in this main room of their small farmhouse, the rugs especially interested the cat. They had a wonderful, woolen smell plus the smell of the kind lady, Bonny.

Pounce rubbed his face against the edges of the rugs draped over the sawhorse, left his own scent on them, and breathed Bonny's scent in again. The floor rugs all had the smell of the dog on them. He didn't like that so he thoughtfully kneaded each one he walked on and left his own cat scent. A closed door on the east side of the living room led to where Matthew and Bonny slept. He had heard their nightly snoring concert and knew Matthew snored the loudest.

His stomach was growling again and he began to wonder when the woman would give him breakfast. At that precise moment the door swung open and the couple entered the room, followed by

Wally. Pounce arched his back and backed up in front of the fireplace and carefully eyed the dog behind the man's legs.

"It's alright, Pounce. Now Wally, you be a good dog and don't hurt my kitty." The woman spoke confidently, but there was a twinge in her voice.

"Caw-err ... Yes, you be a good dog," Pounce growled.

"Hey, cat!" Matthew hollered. "None of that."

Pounce squatted, his ears flattened and his eyes narrow, but he stopped growling.

Wally sat down and considered the cat. Then he cocked his head and said with a huge collie grin, "None of that feline stuff, cat. We're a family here. I'm not going to eat you. The last cat I ate gave me a bellyache and hairballs."

He chuckled good-naturedly. "By the way, pussy cat, I heard you singing in here. You'll not get much dreaming time on those fancy cushions. No, sir, barn duty a-hatching, mice need a-catching, Matthew's plan a-looming, mice need consuming, La, la, la, la, la, la, la." The dog woofed his song in laughter, then plopped down and rolled over on his back by the door still looking over at the cat, his eyes full of amusement.

Pounce was not amused.

"See, Pounce. Wally just wants his belly rubbed. He's a good old boy."

Bonny bent over and stroked the dog, pursing her lips and puffing Wally's name at him. It came out, "Pwally, Pwally, Pwally."

Now it was Pounce's turn. He meowed at the dog. "Ha, yourself, dog. She thinks you're a parrot. Does the Polly-dog want a cracker?"

The meowing sounded friendly like to the farm couple for they did not know that Pounce was mocking the dog. Wally ignored the cat and enjoyed the belly rub. The only things that really upset him were coyotes and rats and other varmints that tried to steal chickens or grain or anything on the farm. He knew his job.

It was to herd cows in and out of the pasture and guard the farm. How people talked, or cats for that matter, didn't bother him. He was a very laid-back collie dog.

Matthew poured his coffee and sat down heavily at the table. "Ah, Ma. They's gotta figure it out for themselves. It'll work down. Now, how about some breakfast?"

"They will, they have to, they must," Bonny softly corrected as she washed her hands at the sink and then began serving the breakfast that waited on several platters in her warm oven.

"Yah, yah. That's what I said," Matthew slurped his coffee loudly and grinned at his wife. He knew what she wanted him to say, but never could think of the right words before he spoke. "That's what I said. They's gotta do it."

Bonny shook her head as Pounce watched her pull something wonderfully smelly out of the oven. It had been still dark when she prepared it an hour earlier and he remembered not being offered anything then but, before he could consider it further, Wally rose and, still grinning impishly at the cat, walked toward him. Pounce arched his back again but didn't move away. Most of what remained of his hair was now lying down.

"Come, cat. I'm a fixture around here. You're going to work in the barn with the other cats. They don't come up to the house. Not allowed. Working types. All the warm milk you can drink. Cows, you know. And then something dry called cat food. Tasty stuff. You'll like it. Mostly meat. Some grain in it."

Wally continued to walk toward Pounce slowly. He talked in his clipped, short way, the words rolling off his tongue in a friendly fashion. He hoped his voice would take the edginess off the little cat.

"You'll like the other cats. Me? I bring cows in and send cows out. I watch the farm. I live in the house. You live in the barn. The folks here are good people. They will feed us and we'll get along."

He stopped a few feet away and looked at Pounce, his head

cocked. The collie smile on his face widened even more while he hummed softly. "Now, take it easy. You must know farm dogs don't eat their cats."

"I'm not your cat!" Pounce hissed low so Matthew wouldn't hear him as Wally put his nose out close to Pounce and was rewarded with a quick cat paw to the side of his face.

"Aw, cat, that wasn't nice. One more time, greet me like you would a neighbor." Wally chuckled, and again he stuck his nose out low and close to Pounce, but now he dropped his belly to the floor and inched forward. This time Pounce allowed his shoulder to be touched by the dog's nose but he was wary. The dog's heavy breathing was distasteful to him.

"You smell like poop," he hissed quietly.

"Yeah. Ain't it grand? Aroma of Randall cattle, I call it. They're the rare cattle kept here on the place. Beats aroma of cat any day." Chuckling again, Wally returned to the rug and dropped heavily.

Okay, Pounce thought. *So, he's not a wild dog and he obeys his master. But be friends with a dog? I don't think so.* Pounce didn't know that it had been a wild coyote that had chased him and not a wild dog for the city cat didn't really know the difference between tame animals that live with people and wild ones that don't. Since his troubles had started, he had only seen a few tame farm animals when he passed through the fields on the edge of town.

While breakfast was being served to Matthew, Pounce flattened himself in front of the fireplace but kept his legs under him, just in case he had to move quickly. It was hard to get his little cat brain around all the things going on presently, and to get out of his brain all the things that had happened to him. He wrinkled his brow anyway and tried to think as clearly as a cat can and this is what he knew so far.

He came from a large, beautiful home that was far away. His

owner was an old, sweet lady named Mom and she loved him. He often slept at the foot of her bed and remembered playing with yarn balls and eating good food, but then things started changing. Mom began to become confused and that troubled Pounce. Some days she forgot to feed him or even herself. One day the man called Son came to the house and called out, "Mom?" But Mom didn't remember her own son for she had become very ill. So that day her whole family came in a big car and took her away.

Several days passed. Pounce was lonely, but he ate the food the man had put down for him, drank from his big dish of water, and continued to sleep on Mom's bed. Then Son came back for him and brought his own son Tom. Pounce was excited and so sure he would be taken to Mom that he purred on the lap of Mom's grandson as they drove. It seemed they went a long way and Pounce happily dozed and purred until they arrived just outside a small town and Son pulled over and parked on the side of the road. He started talking to Tom who had begun to cry and that confused Pounce.

"You'll see, son. Country folks need cats and love them. He will find a new home right away. If we take him to the dog pound at home, they'll put him to sleep."

Pounce didn't think sleep was a bad thing. Being put to sleep in Mom's bed had been very nice but something in the way the man said it caused chills to race down his spine, and he stiffened in the arms of the boy.

"Come on, son, you know the cat can't live where Gram-Mom has to live now and we can't take him. Our apartment manager said no large pets. Your little white mouse is all we're allowed to keep. This is the only way."

"I'm not sure, Dad. Can't we put an ad in the paper, or find others who help find homes for cats, or try a kennel, or something?"

His voice trailed off as his dad firmly lifted Pounce out of his arms and, opening the car door, set him down on the side of the road. The next things Pounce experienced were sharp gravel under his feet, the sound of Tom crying, and the noise and wind from the car driving away.

Pounce was frightened and scurried into the grass by the side of the road and waited. He waited and waited but they never came back. As the days stretched into weeks, Pounce ate scraps he found near garbage cans until people said, "Scat, cat," and chased him away. He grew thinner and hungrier and more tired than he had ever been, and he missed the soft hand of Mom.

One day he saw some boys sitting on their bikes and he walked up to them meowing, hoping they would feed and pet him. Instead they grabbed him, stuffed him into a sack, and rode off with him. It was uncomfortable in the bag, bouncing alongside a bike, held tightly by the riding boy. Pounce cried again and again, but the boys laughed and talked loudly.

Suddenly he was flying out of the bag and through the air as the boys yelled and hooted. Landing on all four feet, he felt pain shoot up his legs as glass cut into his pads. As he hopped about in panic, trying to find a safe place, part of his hair caught on fire and he cried out in terror as heat began to burn his belly and hind legs. Like a worthless sack of garbage, Pounce had been tossed into an open-air, burning garbage dump.

He cried as he scrambled to climb out of the smoldering rubble. He had barely clawed his way out on the other side of the small pit when a bicycle hit him and sent him tumbling again. The boys had followed his progress and tried to knock him back down into the fiery garbage pit, but Pounce rolled and scampered away. It started raining after dark and the weary young cat huddled in the only shelter he could find, a short section of partially crushed road culvert left on the edge of a field.

That first night Pounce coughed and coughed from the smoke he had inhaled. His ribs hurt where the bicycle had hit him. His pads ached from the glass cuts and burns, and the burnt spots on his belly and hind legs made him waddle splay legged when he moved. To lie down in comfort he tried different positions. He curled up on his side, but that made his ribs hurt so he squatted again on his sore pads and lowered his burnt belly to the cold metal of the culvert. That helped a little. No one could hear his pitiful mews with the rain beating hard on the culvert. Pounce could barely hear his own cries.

In the morning, cold and injured, he sat hunched up in the pipe, hesitating to venture out. When he did exit, Pounce found that the wet grass made walking fairly easy as he approached a deep puddle and drank as much water as he could hold. Then, very un-cat-like, he walked in and stood up to his elbows in the water, easing some of his discomfort. Mom had often bathed him so Pounce had no natural fear of shallow water. The cool feel of the water made him think of the cool salve Bonny had rubbed into his feet and he sighed.

Wally studied the sighing cat by the fireplace. It was obvious that he was thinking something and Wally wondered if cats ever think very deeply about important things. Then he answered himself. *No. Cats don't think much.* Shaking his shaggy mane, he lowered his muzzle to the floor again.

Pounce remembered walking through the wet, winter fields until a coyote startled him. It must have been creeping along behind him when suddenly it gave chase. He had a head start but the coyote almost snatched him before he sprang on a watering trough and then leaped again toward the nearest fence post.

His injuries caused him to fall short and he struck the post with his left paw, tumbling into the top strand of the barbed-wire fence. The wire barbs ripped into his hip and he squalled in pain as his weight and forward motion helped him spin free and tumble to the ground on the other side. Scrambling up, he escaped into a thicket and climbed high into the nearest tree. There he panted and waited.

The coyote leaped too but touched a different part of the

fence. He yelped in pain and fell back to the ground. Pounce didn't know why the coyote didn't jump the fence and follow him. It would be a while before he understood that what turned the lights on in the Larsen house and barn also ran through the wire strung just under the top of the barbed wire fence. The electricity in the wire had zapped that coyote good.

All that day and night Pounce stayed in the tree until he felt safe. The next morning he ventured down and crept across several fields by hugging the fence lines. That evening Pounce approached the Larsen farm because he saw lights in the barn. In spite of the mistreatment he'd suffered and the misadventures he'd endured, this thrown away and injured little cat still hoped that someone, somewhere, would help him.

And they are kind. This thought brought his mind to the dog. The Wally dog had cornered him by the barn and then announced the interloper's presence with loud barking. Yet he hadn't bitten or mauled him, he'd only kept him cornered until Bonny had found him huddled in the rain. Bonny had sewed up his wounds and now she was feeding him and petting him every day. He liked her soft ways for she sang as she worked and Pounce loved music.

He thought about loud Matthew and wasn't sure that the big man liked him even though the man had been gentle with him. That term "barn work" unsettled the cat. He didn't know what it meant and he didn't want to learn since he already preferred the house. That's what he understood. His only outside experiences in life had been very, very bad.

Is there housework I can do instead of barn work? He wondered about it, and then turned his thoughts to his sore feet, his sore ribs, and the lack of hair over a good part of his body. Even hunched up on the warm rug, Pounce felt chilled. *My coat.* He moaned and it just barely audible. *My warm, spotted coat,* Pounce sighed and closed his eyes as the good smells of breakfast blew around him. It was so hard to think when there was food nearby and he hoped Bonny would remember to feed him.

Maybe I should have a plan? Cats don't reason well but Pounce tried his best. He shuddered again as the thought of his lost home and lost owner flickered on the edge of his mind. Tears didn't come into his eyes as they do in humans when they think sad thoughts. Instead, Pounce squeaked under his breath. It came out sounding like a tiny hinge needing oil. "Ee–ee–ee." Catching himself, he grew quiet. He didn't want to think about his losses anymore, at least for the moment. Now, all he wanted was a plan.

Wally, lying quietly on his rug, eyed the cat and wondered what his problem was. Wally was a sensitive collie, one with intelligence and some compassion. He heard the low squeak and knew it was animal grief. Wally had learned what human grief was too, and He knew how to make Bonny and Matthew feel better whenever they grew sad looking at the folded flag in the box on the mantle. The dog remembered the tall young man in his new uniform. The boy had been his buddy, and they had played together as they watched each other growing up.

One day the young man had kissed his mother, shaken his father's hand, rumpled Wally's head, and gone away. He hadn't returned. Now, when sadness came into the house, the big dog would lay his head on Matthew and Bonny's knees and gaze into their faces until they petted him and started talking about other things.

When the calves were sold, Wally knew how to comfort the mother cows by just standing alongside, but this cat was different somehow. Though he felt for the naked and wounded cat twitching across the room, Pounce was not one of the barn cats he had been given to guard. So he dismissed any thought of saying something comforting to the cat. *We'll see. We'll see how this ends.* With that thought, Wally blew his breath out loudly and dropped his head once more down on his paws.

Pounce, in the meantime, went on with his attempt to pull the threads of his messed up life into something that made sense. He felt lost and lonely except when Bonny was crooning over him and petting him. *Would he be allowed to live with Bonny in the house?* He hoped so and, with that hope, he fixed his mind on a course to ignore the remarks of the big dog and to work on being permanently assigned to house duty. *I need house duty with soft wool rugs, warm cushions, and fireplace snoozes. House duty. That's my saucer of milk and I aim to drink it. Yes I do!*

With this plan, although it wasn't really much of a plan, Pounce felt better. His cathead was made up. So he sat up and made the signature noise that seemed to please Bonny. To him it was a call for breakfast. To her, it was a musical sound of contentment.

"Purr-ounce. Purr-ounce." He watched as she turned to smile at him and then began to cut up a bit of eggs and bacon for his little dish.

"She likes me," he whispered under his breath, without realizing that the big collie could hear his whisper. Wally rolled over and grinned knowingly as Bonny brought the small dish of food over to Pounce and set it down.

It was Wally's turn to think to himself. *We'll see, you silly, naked little pussycat. Indeed, we'll see.*

CHAPTER 3

Barn Cats

The day, or rather the evening, finally came. After the last chores of the day, Matthew announced that Pounce looked well enough to begin his life in the barn.

"Bring 'em on down to the barn tomorrow morning, Bonny."

Bonny looked at the sleeping cat in her lap and sighed. She knew it was time, but this Pounce cat had a way about him. She enjoyed watching him play at her feet in the evenings, rolling around playing with her yarns and rags. Even though she had to rewind them over and over, she delighted in watching him tumble about with her sewing.

Best of all, she enjoyed his light leap into her lap afterwards that stopped all of her work. Each night Pounce settled down, looked up into her face, smiled with his eyes and began melting her heart with his softest and most contented purr.

Purring should not make me lose my train of thought, she thought. Then she quickly lost that thought as she listened to the Pounce cat purr. The warmth of the cat in her lap, the sounds he made and his silly grinning face looking up at her from his upside down posture, had this mature woman on automatic meltdown. Every night it was the same. The moment the cat settled in her lap, the concerns of the day, the leftover labors, and tomorrow's list of chores vanished away.

Work could not win against the Pounce cat gently kneading his paws on her apron or waving them in the air as she stroked his white belly. So Bonny relaxed, and sometimes even dozed off for a little while.

"You in puddin' mode?" Matthew watched his wife's reaction to the furry thing stretching itself on her lap. "You got a button that cat pushes on ya, wife?"

Bonny's soft chuckle with a slight nod was the only answer he got. The low rumble of the cat combined with the light vibration under her hand as she petted him did put Bonny into something like pudding mode. Her brain cells stopped snapping with any sense and she was content to spend the evening listening to the purr and that was that.

Bonny purred back while she petted him. "Purr, purr, purr." She rolled her "r's" and wished she didn't have to catch a breath after every two or three "purr's." "How do they do that inside, Matthew? How do they purr while they are breathing?"

Matthew dropped into his chair beside Bonny and put up his tired feet. "Ah, how do I know? Ain't never heard such talk. They just do, that's all."

Though preoccupied by the farm work, the man could not ignore his life-long partner. Years had come and gone and still she loved him and he knew it. Matthew did not purr or talk to cats. Nor was he soft. Some thought his loud ways meant he was harsh, but Bonny knew better. He was simply Matthew, a hard-working, brutally honest, and thoroughly good man. When he was a younger man, he'd heard their preacher say that God wanted men to be good. So he was. That was Matthew. His wife and animals were safe with him.

"Oh Matthew, you old fuddy-duddy," Bonny said warmly. "You like this cat. I know you do."

"Yeah, yeah, but honey, it's a cat. I know where this talk is goin'. This Pounce cat of yours belongs in the barn with the rest of 'em. We can't have a worthless house cat. He's gotta earn his keep like everythin' else around here."

Bonny sighed and hugged Pounce on her lap tighter. He liked it. And though he pretended to be a dozing, purring cat, he was actually very alert and listening to every word.

"Bonny, I ain't said much yet, for the poor puss was bad hurt. But now he's well and he's gotta go out. You ain't gettin' much rug work done at night any more. That cat," Matthew stabbed the air with his finger at the cat, "takes up your whole evenin'. You know how much we get for your wool rugs. Why we could sell these under our feet even now, they're so fine. Sellin' the wool rugs adds to our retirement fund. Ain't a lot maybe, but havin' some-thing' just for savings 'n not depending' on cow and hay markets is more'n most farmers got around here and that cat's gettin' in the way of it. Besides, how many jars of pickles can you sell to make up for one grand rug? Ha!"

Matthew's loud laugh with the pickle point was not new. He used it at various times during the year because of his wife's great love for pickle making and his not so great interest in eating any-thing that was pickled. Yet Bonny knew it was Matthew's way of letting her know that love prevailed in spite of the cat, or the pickles for that matter.

Pounce listened intently. *So, she made all these beautiful rugs. Her attention to me is getting in the way of my house plan.* Pounce purred louder and rolled over the other direction in her lap, show-ing more white belly hair. She rubbed it while he thought. *What if I did something that was important to the man? Something the barn cats can't do and something the Wally dog has never thought of doing? Now what would it be? I've got to think it up quick before get-ting put out.*

Pounce started getting excited as he developed his plan. Of course Pounce didn't really have a plan, he just figured that if he thought long enough, he would come up with one. However the petting kept getting in the way of his thinking and so, with-out thinking any more, he stretched and then started kneading the air as Bonny rubbed his belly. Finally he spoke his signature sound and she loved it. "Purr-ounce. Purr-ounce."

"See, Bonny, he's already a pest."

"No, Matthew, he's just enjoying his belly rub. And look how well he's healed on his hip too. But don't you think his coat's still a bit short for outside? We snipped him close you know, and I think it's too cold at night for him in the barn yet."

"Huh." The grunt spoke volumes and Bonny and Pounce both knew they had him.

"Okay. But just a little longer while his coat grows out."

Pounce and Bonny sighed at the same time.

"But he's still gotta go outside during the warm part of the day since he's gotta meet the cats and chickens and such and I've gotta see if'n he's aggressive to any of 'um too."

Pounce lifted his upside down head and rolled over in Bonny's lap to get a good long look at Matthew. *Live chickens? We didn't have those in town. They're tasty. Bonny's chopped chicken, gravy and milk, oh my white boots, that's good.* Just the thought of the dinner he'd already eaten sent Pounce into a dream state. He went limp and forgot that he needed to develop a plan for staying in the house. Instead, he began to sing.

"Ah, gravy, gravy, lovely chicken gravy." Pounce sang to himself through his purr. It was a different sound than his normal purr. He was vocalizing through the purr and the couple could hear both closed mouth cat meows and purring at the same time.

Like a delighted child, Bonny giggled and continued to stroke the cat. "Listen, Matthew. Pounce is singing." Bonny giggled again with the jolly light sound that fit her well. She was generally a contented soul who took pleasure in small gifts. This injured cat singing through his purr was a personalized evening lap concert just for her. She couldn't have been happier.

Matthew didn't look up or answer. He just settled deeper into his chair and made several low "huh" sounds through puffed out lips as he shook his heavy jowls back and forth. Pounce went on singing. Some of the gravy words came out sounding like *bravey, bravey,* as Pounce sang. But he didn't care. It was his song and he sang it joyfully.

> "Gravy, gravy,
> Oh, lovely chicken gravy,
> I would swim all day and night through it.
> Gravy, gravy,
> Oh, lovely chicken gravy,
> I'll join the chicken navy
> Just to get some lovely gravy
> For the taste of chicken gravy makes me
> Feel right fit."

Suddenly, Bonny remembered where Matthew had left off talking and she answered him. "All right, Matthew, I'll do it. Pounce goes outside during the warm part of the day. But if he looks miserable, I'll bring him in again."

Matthew sighed this time, "Right, Bonny. Right."

The following day, true to her word, Bonny carried Pounce outside and set him down on the step. "Come on, Pounce. I'm going for eggs and you must meet the cats." Pounce walked carefully down the steps and out into the yard. It seemed bigger than he remembered from the night Bonny carried him across it into the house.

They crossed a grassy area and then a gravel area. The stones were a little hard on his feet and Bonny noticed him walking gingerly. The big barn door was open and Pounce could hear animal sounds from inside. He had barely stepped inside when two yellow cats jumped directly down in front of him off a stall door.

"These are the Yellow Boys, Pounce. They catch a lot of mice but aren't too good at rats yet. Now, be good to Pounce, boys. He lives here." Bonny spoke sharply and wagged a finger at the Yellow Boys, then continued walking back into the depths of the barn.

The chicken house was just outside the big sliding door in the back of the barn. Bonny never could understand why Matthew built the chicken house so far away from her garden. It just didn't make sense to her. Bonny wanted to gather eggs at the same time she pulled a few onions out of the ground or whacked off a head of lettuce for dinner. Even Matthew's explanations didn't change her mind.

"Honey, chicken yards don't smell good and they gotta be far away from the house; 'n pigs don't smell good either and that's why they is down there too."

She grimaced as she walked through the barn. Her jolly nature was pinched a bit as she thought about where she really wanted the chicken house, but she knew it would never be moved. So she let the thought go for that also was a part of her good nature. Disappointments did not cause her to think less of her dear Matthew. After the good thought had replaced the pinched, she walked on happily, humming to herself. Bonny was content. *Matthew, my dear Matthew, thirty-five years I've been gathering eggs for your breakfast.*

Then Bonny chuckled and the sweetness of her nature rose fully to the surface with a fresh thought. *Omelets. I'll make the best fresh egg omelet he ever tasted.* Bonny dipped a pail into the cracked corn barrel just inside the back door of the barn and then quickened her steps as she went outside and turned toward the chicken house. "Here, chick, chick, chick," she called.

Pounce took note that the Yellow Boys were not good with rats. *I might need that bit of information later.* It was a rare sensible thought for a cat, but Pounce didn't dwell on it. His mental prowess fled as he also noted that these cats were not called by their names. Pounce was back to surface thinking about what was in front of him for just their color was mentioned and he wondered about that.

They were not really yellow, but mostly muddy white and

cream cats with pale yellow spots all over their fur. One cat had pale green eyes and the other one had pale yellow eyes. Other than the eyes and the placement of several pale yellow spots, they were practically identical. *Everything about them is pale,* Pounce thought, *but one is a little bigger.* He studied them as they studied him in return. The Yellow Boys lifted their fur and drew closer to Pounce and then they began to circle him and growl.

"We don't need another cat. Scat. Scat, cat!" This last part was hissed at Pounce. They were so close he could feel the spray of their spit and he didn't like it a bit.

"Oh, you boys are poets? I'll give you some real poetry," Pounce growled in return as he lifted what was left of his coat and arched his back. Then he instantly stopped. *Oops, that sounded aggressive. Bonny won't like a catfight. All right, I'll play weak. These yellow fur balls won't know the difference.* Pounce promptly fell over on his side and offered the Yellow Boys his belly. He closed his eyes and waited. *I can handle a nip or two without retaliating. I just hope they don't bite the sore hip. Maybe I should have fallen on the other side.*

The Yellow Boys stopped growling and began sniffing Pounce. He lay still and closed his eyes tight. They touched what was left of his hair with their paws and breathed the breath of his nose. They studied the stitches on his hip and the scars on his side. They even sniffed his bare legs where the pit fire had singed him and examined all the areas where Bonny had cut off his coat.

"Boy, you're one beat-up cat. We could finish it, you know!" The largest one of the two yellow cats pawed at Pounce's side as he spoke.

"Yeah, we is in charge around here." The smaller cat meowed this last volley into Pounce's closest ear.

"We are in charge around here. You should have said we are, not we is, but even though your grammar would be correct, your position would not. You are not in charge around here. I am." This last was said in a low, firm cat voice. "Your turn, yellow pusses. Scat!"

Pounce raised his head to look for the owner of that lovely, yet authoritative voice.

As he did, the Yellow Boys slunk down the barn alley and in their place Pounce saw a vision, and what a vision it was.

The most beautiful feline he had ever seen walked into his line of sight. Her walk was slow and feminine and seemed to flow as she placed one dainty front paw in front of the other. Her long, upright tail waved gently. Pounce had never seen such a coat. She was a silver-grey tabby with lovely, wide, dark grey and light silver stripes all over her body, some of them swirling in circles on her sides. Her eyes were green and penetrating and she was smiling at him.

Pounce shook his head in wonder. *Could this be? This lovely creature lives in the barn and I want to be a house cat? Oh Mama kitty. What's your boy to do?* He longed to touch her thick shiny coat, but that would have been inappropriate as they had not really met, and he didn't know her name.

"Hello there. You must not mind the Yellow Boys. They can be obnoxious, but they do kill their share of mice and occasionally even a snake or two. They will leave you alone, most of the time." She smiled. "You must be Pounce. Welcome. I'm Catcher."

By this time Pounce was sitting up and staring as she walked directly in front of him and sat down. She put her head forward and touched the end of his nose with her own, giving him a proper and polite cat greeting.

"Oh, my. You have been in the house. You smell of cooked chicken and I'll bet you had raw eggs whipped up for you. Yes?"

"Yeees," Pounce croaked out. "Yes," he said the second time firmly, while still staring into her deep green eyes.

"It's all right, Pounce. I'm a cat just like you and I understand why you are staring. You think me pretty, don't you?"

Pounce looked away suddenly.

"Don't be embarrassed, Pounce. I used to be a valuable show

cat; that is, until one particular cat show." Catcher smiled and took a deep breath before continuing. "I'm called an American Shorthaired Silver Classic Tabby. That's a lot of words to heap on one little kitty, isn't it?" She giggled and Pounce quickly looked back and saw that her eyes were now a light mint in color and sparkling. He was completely entranced.

"I'll tell you my story, Pounce; it will help us get acquainted. At this cat show, and across from where the other shorthairs and I were caged, were the Siamese cats. One started talking to me across the row. He was older than me and had won many ribbons in cat shows. They hung all over his box.

"I was young and had won several ribbons too. So when he wanted to talk to me, I was flattered and felt honored too. The Siamese cat was strong and handsome. And I? I was young and foolish. I should have listened to my mother. She told me not to talk to strangers, but," Catcher sighed as she talked, "I forgot."

Pounce squatted down in front of her and looked up at her shiny silver chin as she told her story.

"Later the Siamese's owner opened his cat's cage door. I was sitting in my open cage too. Our owners were not paying attention. They were too busy talking about the cat show when this bold cat jumped across the aisle to talk some more to me. He told me to hop down and go for a walk, but I said that I was supposed to stay put. He kept urging me and at first I wanted to go, but I knew I shouldn't. Then I started feeling uncomfortable as he kept talking. So I stood up and told him firmly that I had to stay put. He got pushy and pawed at me, so I hissed and told him to go away. My hiss must have angered him for with one fast leap which I barely saw coming," she sighed again, "he raked and bit me, ripping into my leg deeply in several places. It really hurt."

Catcher was silent and Pounce held his breath, waiting for the next part of her story.

"I cried out and our owners pulled us apart as he kept clawing me. I can still hear the angry screams from that Siamese as he was carried away. He probably always got his own way and wouldn't take no for an answer," Catcher again paused in the telling.

Another minute went by while Pounce tried to remember to breathe. Catcher looked at the straw on the barn floor as if she were not in the middle of her compelling tale. She looked up finally and caught Pounce's wide eyes staring at her.

"My owner picked me up, but as soon as he saw that I was torn and bleeding, his face changed. Then he said lots of nasty words to the Siamese's owner, words that I must never repeat and I hope that someday will never, ever, come back into my mind."

Pounce was fascinated by everything she said, and puzzled by what some of it meant. But he kept listening and tried to breathe and keep his mouth closed at the same time. He was suddenly very aware at how little he knew about the world.

"I thought my owner would call the veterinarian to look at my hurt leg. But instead, he started packing everything up and loaded me in my kennel for the trip home. At least that's where I thought we were going. My leg hurt, and the injuries were just too deep for me to lick and make them feel better. When we passed through the countryside on the way back home, my owner stopped at this farm and offered me to Matthew to become a barn cat.

"That's when Bonny took me into the house and nursed me back to health just like she did you. She sewed my leg up like she did your hip. See?" At this Catcher raised one beautiful hind leg and licked the fur open on the inside of it. Slurp. Slurp. The wet fur separated, exposing a long crooked scar and several smaller jagged ones.

"My owner would not keep what he called damaged goods in his family of cats. That is what he told Matthew and Bonny and that's what I had become."

Catcher said this last part slowly with her eyes lowered. "I never saw my friends and family again. Especially I miss my owner's wife. Her name was Anna and she loved me."

Pounce felt almost dizzy with shock. Thoughts hit his mind and stung. It felt like the gravel that had sprayed back against him when Son had left him on the side of the road and driven away. *Pop, pop, pop.* The gravel pummeled his mind. He had lost his beloved owner too, not because he was plain to look at, though he was, but because she was too old to care for him anymore. He remembered when Son took her away and afterwards how it felt to be torn out of the arms of the boy and dumped out of the car. *Pop. Pop. Pop.* The memory made him shake with fear all over once again.

"Are you all right?" he heard Catcher ask.

He came back from his inward journey, nodded his head in a yes and tried to think again about Catcher's story. *This gorgeous vision has been injured like me. She has suffered and then been thrown away too. Just like me. Like we have no value.* Pounce hung his head and then shook it as he felt first sadness and then anger rise in him.

Some of his mother's words began to come back to him as he continued to slowly shake his head from side to side. His mother told him that rough and tumble boy cats get scars sometimes. Then she said that little girl cats should have someone in the family to watch out for them, because someday they would grow up to be mothers, and it was important to respect your mother.

Following that advice in the few short months he lived at home with his brothers and sisters, he and his brothers had learned to watch over their sisters as though they were being respectful of their mother. At the time all the boys complained and didn't want to do it. They thought it a silly game, and that their mother was just old fashioned and didn't know that girls were as tough as boys. And besides, the girls didn't want to be treated differently. It was not a pleasant lesson at the time for his mama boxed the boys' ears when they were rough with their sisters.

Now he was almost a grown-up cat and, as he listened to this beautiful creature talking to him, suddenly he was sure that mama had been right. *Girls need protection and respect. But who had protected and respected Catcher?*

He growled under his breath and blew his breath out harshly. Then Pounce narrowed his eyes against every Siamese cat in the whole world, even the good ones, although he was sure there could not be any good ones. He'd never met a Siamese cat and he did not know exactly what one looked like, but Pounce was sure, absolutely sure, he would know one if it ever came around.

Then he growled another low growl against cat owners that took cats to shows though he wasn't real sure what a cat show was, or if all other owners were like Catcher's owner or not.

Pounce was an ordinary cat with average intelligence and a limited exposure to the world. However, he was passionate in what he believed and loyal to what he had learned from his mother about right and wrong. Some of his views were untested, since at this point in his youthful life he had very little exposure to anything evil except, of course, people who throw away pets, young men who are mindlessly cruel, and coyotes who try to kill cats.

Now, he had heard of another evil done to a cat and he was shocked by it. It had not occurred to him that other cats went through troubles like what he had endured. As his mother's words came back to him, he remembered what she had taught the kittens. *Right is to be loyal to your family and friends. Wrong is to cast away family and friends when they become burdensome, or when they don't further your personal goals.*

Pounce knit the bond of friendship instantly when he saw Catcher's injuries and heard her story. His good mother would have been pleased. So he focused on Catcher again, growled low in his throat one more time to show his support for his new friend, but then looked abruptly away from her beautiful, stretched-out leg and stared instead at the nearest stall door.

There were large calves moving around inside so Pounce pretended to have suddenly become interested in their sounds. Besides, the calves sounded alarming even though they were behind the heavy wood planking of their stall. Pounce had never been this close to a large animal before. Catcher saw the change in his countenance and how he looked away. She was charmed by his good manners.

"It's okay, Pounce. It happened when I was a bit younger and I'm grown up now and happy here. Oh, the Yellow Boys are pesky sometimes, but Bonny pets me every day and I have a good life. It's a more natural life than I could have had as a show cat. Do you know how show cats live? Do you even know what a show cat is?"

Pounce wanted to say yes, but he honestly shook his head no and fixed his eyes on her lovely face again. Her whiskers moved animatedly as she talked and he found himself captivated by the movement.

"Show cats are supposed to win lots of trophies for their owners. Many live in locked up little cages that are in places called catteries. They are taken out to be exercised and bathed and groomed and then are locked up again."

"Locked up? In a cage?"

"That's the way it was for me, at least for a while, until my owner's wife took a liking to me and often let me run around the house and sit on her lap. She read to me and talked to me and petted me too."

"I know. Me too! My owner did the same thing."

Pounce's interruption didn't seem to bother Catcher, and he was glad they had similar backgrounds. He blinked back happily at his new friend, but wondered at the slow smile that played around Catcher's face as she studied him.

"I was an investment for my owner and not a pet," Catcher continued, "but his wife loved me. To him, my future was to be a winner in the show ring, then a mama to kittens. My best kittens would have been taken to cat shows by my owner, or would have been sold."

Catcher narrowed her eyes and they turned a dark green as she remembered the past. Her look was intense for a moment, and then suddenly she lay down with her front legs stretched out in front of her. The morning light was now casting stripes across the barn's entry as it fell on stall partitions and on the cats.

Pounce was startled to see how bright Catcher's silver stripes were when the sun hit them. They flashed shiny rays back again as her coat turned from dark silver in the shadows to sparkling silver in the sunlight and he was more than slightly captivated; he was besotted. Catcher's attractiveness and warm personality had Pounce in a confused state of mind. He was smitten, but didn't know quite what had happened.

"I'd much rather be here in a drafty barn then in my master's cattery," Catcher said with heat. Then the green orbs lightened once more to their bright inviting color as she finished her story. "This is a good life for me now. The only bright spot in my old life was my owner's wife. I still miss her sometimes."

Catcher looked over at Pounce and smiled a warm, slit-eye cat smile. It was a long speech and Pounce was quite taken aback by it all. He tried to remember everything she had said, but could not and even his anger against unknown Siamese cats had melted away. Pounce leaned forward suddenly and touched her nose.

"I'm sorry," he said.

"Thank you, Pounce. "Now, though it's warming up today, it's still cool out here and Bonny may let you go back into the house to keep warm," she said softly. "Your coat will grow in and cover the patches and scars. I think I can tell that you are a good looking sort of cat, or at least you will be when you have hair again."

Her smile told him she was teasing. "I've heard the humans talk about you out here. Bonny wants you in the house. Matthew wants you in the barn. We'll see how it falls out. In the meantime, I like you. We have much to talk about."

"Okay, I'd like that."

"Later I will take you around the farm and explain everything. You must meet all the animals. There are places for you to go and some places that you must never go."

This last bit of information was delivered as Catcher looked directly into Pounce's eyes and he felt the statement to his core. It was unnerving but he didn't know why. He stood up, glanced toward the barn door and then looked again to the beautiful silver cat standing in the shafts of sunlight. Catcher's dark silver and black tail waved slowly behind her as though urging him to go. *What an interesting way to say good-bye,* Pounce thought, completely missing the point that she was showing pleasure in their new friendship.

This missed point may have saved the younger cat from embarrassment for he still wanted to touch that shiny coat. It didn't seem real that a cat could be such a beauty and still be a cat. Pounce's knowledge of the world was expanding.

"Soon?"

"Yes, Pounce. Soon."

He turned again and walked up toward the house. That evening it seemed that everywhere he looked something was reflecting light back at him. The kettle on the stove, the glasses in the dish rack, the candlesticks on the fireplace mantel all caught his attention and made him think of silver swirling stripes on a lovely girl cat. That night he had dreams of Catcher's deep green eyes. He seemed to be falling into them.

CHAPTER 4

Kittens in the Hole

It was Saturday and that meant going-to-town day. Matthew was especially loud and cheerful. "Breakfast early, my dear. We'll need to get a-goin' right after milkin'."

Pounce stirred in his dresser bed and watched the early morning hustle. Standing up and stretching one end of his body at a time, he sat down again and yawned. *Ah, that feels good. Yes, breakfast.* Pounce licked his lips in anticipation as the smell of frying bacon and sizzling eggs drifted over him. Hopping down, he hurried to stand at Bonny's feet. "Bur-ree-eow? Bur-ree-eow?" He asked politely, in his nicest breakfast call.

"Aha, Pounce. You've got to wait. Matthew first and you can have the leftovers."

Just then Wally wagged his way into the kitchen followed by Matthew. "Clear, warm day, Bonny. Truck ready. Chores done. Let's eat."

"Yes, let's eat." Wally was panting heavily as he lay down on the rug next to Matthew's chair.

"Eat? You're getting fat, dog. Puffing this early in the morning." Pounce mocked the dog foolishly for he felt cocky. Catcher had talked to him the day before and it made him feel very boy-cat strong.

"Silence, cat. You didn't get up in the dark, walk the pasture to look for predators, and drive the cows out after milking. Nor did you put the unruly bull back in his corral and then take the horses down to the river pasture."

It was obvious that Pounce's remark had not set well with Wally who growled his answer toward Pounce without looking at him. Pounce instantly cowered, looked down at the floor, and did not say anything else just as Bonny set a big plate of eggs and bacon with a mound of fried potatoes in front of Matthew.

"Wonderful girl. Good cook. I'll keep you." The loud man lifted several slices of fat bacon off his plate and fed them to Wally.

"Matthew!" Bonny corrected him with a smile and added, "Wally can wait."

"You shoulda seen 'um, Bonny. That young bull is a handful. I couldn't get the rope on his halter he was pushin' me so hard. Then he charged out of his holdin' pen. Another two cracked poles. One's really gone. The other one I can trim, but I gotta make his pen a lot stronger for sure. You shoulda seen it. Our Wally went like a bullet and had the big boy workin' in the field like a sheep on show day. It was somethin' to behold, my girl. Such a lota barkin' and snortin' and me justa hollerin'."

Matthew shouted in excitement even above his usual volume as he shoveled a huge forkful of potatoes in his mouth and growled around it. "You didn't hear us?"

"No, my dear. No. Are you okay?"

"Yah, yah. I'm fine. Once Wally brought him back to the pen, that bull he was a-huffin' and a-puffin' and ready for me to tie him up. By the time I ran another couple poles into the broken fence, I thought you'd a-eaten my breakfast. What a mornin'!"

Matthew stuffed his mouth with eggs and toast and fried potatoes while washing great mouthfuls down with hot coffee and still, somehow, kept the story flowing. "Gotta work with that young bull more. Can't have a wild bull on the place. He's a good 'un and good enough to show, I think. Old Brownie was not this good. My, we're gonna have us some pretty calves."

"That's real fine, dear. Now relax a bit while I clean up the kitchen and we'll be off."

Matthew reached out to pound Wally on the back with his big hand. "Ha, Wall! Today you get to meet the Anderson's little collie bitch. Prettiest gold and white girl you'll ever likely see. You'll like that, yah?"

Wally raised his head to look at his master as Bonny scraped most of the leftover breakfast into a pan, added some dried dog food to it and put it on the floor by the door for Wally whose muzzle quickly dropped into his own breakfast.

Bonny added a few bites of eggs and chopped bacon to a handful of dried cat food and put it down for Pounce, but he was now feeling something besides hunger and didn't move toward his dish. Pounce kept his head down and felt something akin to shame. He had just mocked the big dog that had caught a bull for these kind people who were nursing him back to health. He thought a moment and then did something cats never do. Meowing a soft apology to the dog, he rolled over and showed his belly to the collie.

"Meow, Meow," he called softly toward Wally.

Wally finished licking his plate clean before answering the cat. "Okay, cat. You're still new. You don't know much. But you must learn to find out the truth first. Before you talk." Wally turned to Pounce with his old, friendly collie look. Then he repeated his last words, "Before you talk."

Pounce nodded slowly and closed his eyes as he stood over his bowl. Mama kitty was right. *Sorry isn't too hard a word to say even if it is a bit embarrassing.* Pounce ate slowly, still in thought, until Bonny suddenly scooped him up.

"Outside, Pounce. Today we go to town and you explore the farm. And since you are so slow this morning, you pussycat you, I'll put your breakfast outside on the porch. See? Now eat it all, you sweet little thing."

Matthew groaned at his wife's foolishness but took her by the arm and smiled down at his little round wife. To him, she was the *sweet little thing*, not the cat. A short time later Matthew's pick-up truck pulled away with Wally in the back.

Pounce arrived at the barn where Catcher was waiting. "Come. See what all the fuss is about this morning." She hurried off and Pounce trotted after her, sure he was being taken out to see the bull. Catcher led him down the aisle and around a corner into what looked like a small hall. It was tucked halfway down the barn and opened up into an area that held saddles, ropes, rakes, chains, and all sorts of farm tools. There was even a horse cart by a large door with its shafts laid over the top of some straw bales. Harnesses hung overhead on the wall alongside horse collars. Pounce didn't recognize most of the things or know what they were used for. He stopped suddenly when he heard tiny mews.

"Come on, Pounce. This is a great day around here." She led him forward to some straw bales loosely stacked in the corner by the side door. The mews were coming from somewhere in the pile. A black cat suddenly thrust her head up out of the stack followed by her thin body and fierce growls. Pounce backed up, startled, but Catcher kept walking.

"Hi again, Blackie. This is Pounce. He came here injured and was sewn up by Bonny. And for now he's living in the house until his hair grows out."

"Hiss," Blackie replied staring angrily at Pounce. "Hiss," she said again and then continued in rhyme.

> "Hiss! No strange cats are allowed in here,
> No closer now, you better fear,
> I'm a mom with kittens dear
> And no strange cats are allowed in here. Hiss!"

Blackie continued to spit at Pounce even after speaking.

"Oh. You say poetry too? That was beautiful." He smiled

slowly as he spoke and sat down, fervently hoping she would understand that he meant no harm.

"Blackie had kittens last night. All the animals know about it, but not Matthew." Catcher giggled her news as her green eyes flashed with excitement. "Even Wally couldn't get Matthew to come and look. Too busy with that dumb bull, I guess."

"Kittens? Congratulations on your family. I trust they are well?"

Blackie glowered at him, but began to reconsider her first impression of this injured cat. She was a simple wild cat who, without benefit of a wholesome upbringing or any kind of good education, still had a poetic soul. It often came out of her in rhyme or in verses when she spoke, and always when she sang.

The feral cat softened her thoughts toward Pounce and watched him closely. *This hairless wonder likes poetry? Perhaps he won't hurt new kittens like many male cats do.*

In Blackie's mind, poetry and gentleness went together. She ignored the fact that her most recent poem was spoken with snarls and hisses, but then cats are often unreasonable and especially protective mama cats.

"Blackie is kind of new here too, Pounce. She is what is called a feral cat."

Pounce looked at Blackie thoughtfully and wondered what kind of show cat that was.

"No, no, Pounce." Catcher smiled, as she seemed to read his mind. "Feral means wild. Blackie has never been in a house, or been touched by human hands though somewhere in the past she had tame grandparents, but she was born outside like all wild cats are."

"Never touched?" The tone in Pounce's voice revealed his surprise.

"You got a problem with that, hey, boy?" Blackie put her ears half down as a slight snarl flattened her whiskers.

"No, ma'am. No problem at all. I just never heard of a cat born outside."

That seemed to do it. Blackie flopped over on the straw bale and laughed. "Where'd you get this scratched up, patched up one, Catch? Ha, ha, ha."

"I know, Blackie. It takes all kinds. This one's the champion of innocence."

Both girls were now laughing, but Pounce caught Catcher winking at him so he knew that everything was going to be just fine. When the girl talk had subsided, Catcher drew a bit closer to Blackie and sat down on another bale and began to lick her front paws.

"Do you think it would be alright if I show Pounce your beautiful new kittens?" she asked gently.

"Yeah, yeah. Just not too close, Boyo! Righto?" This last was not really a question, but an order.

"Yes, ma'am," Pounce answered respectfully. "I'll keep my distance. And thank you, ma'am."

Pounce didn't say Blackie's name when he addressed her because his mother had raised him to respect age, and he could see that Blackie was a much older cat than he or Catcher. He also knew not to assume a more familiar relationship with new acquaintances than he had, leaving such things to develop in a natural way.

Pounce's old-fashioned courtesy amazed Blackie for this was a trait seldom found in the feral cat colonies she had visited, but one that she liked. So a touch of acceptance began to form on her hard features and her whiskers moved forward with the hint of a smile as she watched him. Her nerves were now calm and the snarls and hisses were all forgotten.

Pounce sprang up to the same bale with Catcher and then carefully peered down into a hole formed by the way the loose straw bales were stacked. He caught his breath when he saw the seven little mewing balls of hair. They were so tiny and of so many different colors. Three of them were black like their mother. One was white and brown and red with some grey and black too. He had never seen a kitten colored like that before. A couple of them were striped grey and black, and the last one was solid grey all over, except for its little white feet.

The kittens were shiny and wet and he rightly guessed that Blackie had just washed them. Their eyes were tightly shut and they jerked erratically as they attempted to move around. Pounce sighed with delight. "Wow. Kittens. I've never seen any except my own brothers and sisters. Was I that tiny?"

Blackie laughed. "You must a-been a pampered house cat, hey? And a poet cat, wouldn't ya say? Hey, hey?" Blackie spit it out but she was no longer angry. It was just the way she talked.

Pounce jumped down to the barn floor with a "Thank you, ma'am."

And now with the kitten visiting accomplished, Catcher hopped down also. "See you later, Blackie. I must show this Pounce cat the farm animals."

"Yeah, yeah. Scato. See ya later, Kiddo Cato."

When they were out of Blackie's hearing, Pounce quietly asked about one of the kittens. "About that special kitten?"

"Which one, Pounce?"

"That spotted one. You know, the one with white and brown and red and black and such?"

Catcher's face twitched with amusement. "No, my city friend, that is not a special kitten. It's just a different colored one. Under their coat colors, they are all the same. The color of their hair is just different, that's all."

"But, but the way it looked?" Pounce's voice trailed off. He was puzzled.

"Pounce, looks are looks and everyone has them. We just look different on the outside. That's all. Looks are not on the inside. That kitten is a she. Most cats colored like that are called tortoise-shells, and almost all of them are girl cats. My first owner didn't like them and said they looked like pieces dumped out of a puzzle box. He said someone put them together all wrong."

Pounce suddenly remembered his owner working over a box of highly colored cardboard pieces on her card table. She always let him watch from her lap, his head resting on the lip of the card table.

"His wife though, she told her husband that God was the 'somebody' who put them together. She said my owner was just prejudiced against tortoiseshells and other things too."

"What's prejudiced?"

"I'm not real sure, Pounce. But the way she said it, I guess it means that you don't like someone for a silly reason, or for no reason at all."

Catcher laughed a little and Pounce joined in. Then his thoughts went back to the kittens. "They are so little and, and ..."

"And cute?"

"Yes, I guess so, that too. I was thinking more of how little and, and vulnerable." He stuttered a bit over the big word, remembering how easily his old owner had used it.

"Good boy, Pounce. I'm glad to see that you are a sensible enough cat to recognize the needs of, as you say, vulnerable kittens. I didn't know you knew a word that big."

"My owner used to read out loud and I listened from her lap while she petted me. That's when I learned a lot of words for she was an old lady and very smart. But I don't remember prejudiced. Maybe she didn't read that one."

He smiled with pleasure as he remembered and widened his eyes. Then he saw a twinkle in Catcher's shiny green eyes. It gave him a funny warm feeling and, at the same time, it unsettled him a bit.

As they walked, Catcher told Pounce how hard Blackie's life had been until the day she wandered by the barn. "Matthew keeps grain as feed for the chickens and livestock so lots of mice come around, and sometimes rats come too. Blackie started hunting close by, and soon she was hunting in the barn after Matthew went back into the main house for the night. After a while he glimpsed her carrying off a mouse or two early in the morning so he started putting down milk, table scraps, and then a little dry cat-food.

"Soon she decided to stay and now we have another mouser and the farm has a litter of seven new kittens. Isn't it grand?" Catcher's eyes shone with excitement at the idea of the tiny kittens in the barn. "I know Matthew well enough to say that he won't let Blackie raise them to be wild. You watch. He'll get his hands on them soon enough. I hope Blackie doesn't scoot off with them into the woods."

"Why? They're her kittens."

"Oh, Pounce, you really don't know, do you?" Catcher spoke slowly, with the full intent that Pounce should learn the ways of nature fast.

"No doubt most of her kittens would not survive in the wild. They are too little to feed themselves and too slow to keep up with their mama. And what if they ran into danger? I didn't ask, but it's unlikely that all of Blackie's brothers and sisters survived. Remember your brush with the coyote? Lots of other things are out there too and I've seen weasels, and owls, and hawks. There's lots of danger in the wild. I do hope Blackie can be reasoned with when Matthew and Bonny discover the kittens."

"Oh. I've not seen any of those other animals."

"Well, you will, my housebound friend. You will. And I'm here to help you adjust to your life in the barn and teach you how to make a life out here. Bonnie told me to watch over you."

Pounce sighed inwardly. There it was again. That unwelcome reference to his upcoming life in the barn. He was confused for he was beginning to feel something warm toward Catcher. When he saw her, he wanted to spend lots of time with her. It was a feeling that competed with his desire to be a house cat. *Oh, that nice bed and chicken gravy.* Pounce licked his lips at the thought of gravy as he walked back slowly alongside Catcher to the open barn door.

"Come on, Pounce. It's going to take most of the day to meet the bull and the chickens. Then we need to sit on the fence over-looking the pasture behind the chicken coop too."

"What for?"

Catcher giggled. "To listen for mice along the fence, silly. The field mice like to sneak out of the field and steal chicken feed, and it's the cats' work to catch them in the act. It's a lot of fun. You'll see. Then this evening you will meet the cows and horses when they come in from pasture. And the sow too, but we'll not get close to her. I'm told sows can be dangerous. We'll do all this, that is, if Bonny hasn't taken you back to your soft bed."

Pounce suddenly remembered that Catcher had also been nursed in the house and had once been a fancy show cat. She had always been in a house and never free to run around outside. The thoughts whirled around in his head. *How did she make the transition, and why did she seem to like it so? Doesn't she miss the house and Bonny?* He didn't ask those questions. Instead, he quickly picked up on one word she'd said. "Sow?"

"A sow is a female pig. You know, bacon and ham? I could smell it on you when you came down this morning. You've been eating bacon again."

"Oh, yeah. I didn't know it came from pigs though."

Catcher tried unsuccessfully not to giggle again. "Oh, Pounce. You are so much fun, so honest, and so ignorant at the same time. What did you eat when you lived in the city with the old lady?"

"Cat food. It came out of a tin and was delicious and there were different flavors. She always read the label to me and asked me to choose the one I wanted. Of course I can't read, but I nosed the tin I thought was fish and it often was. I was especially fond of whitefish and tuna, and I'd never tasted dry cat food until coming to the farm. Mom ..."

"Mom?"

"Yes. That's what her son called her, so I called her that too. She didn't feed me much of her food. Well, sometimes I'd get a piece of meat or fish that she couldn't finish herself. Oh, the poached fish was the best."

Pounce got a dreamy look on his silly black and white face. It made Catcher smile inwardly as she watched his whiskers twitch in memory. Catcher was a rare cat in that she had discovered how to find pleasure in ordinary things, especially in her companions and their differences.

Pounce didn't take offense when he heard her low giggle at some of his words. He wasn't sure what made her laugh, but he was having too much fun walking beside this silver tabby, this beautiful and wise silver tabby, to take offense.

They were now outside the barn and starting around the side when Catcher stopped suddenly. They both stiffened as the smell of something unpleasant reached their nostrils.

"Pounce. Quick. Follow me." Catcher raced back to the open barn door and scrambled to get up onto the woodshed that ran alongside the barn on the side facing the house. Pounce was close at her heels. In a whisker of time, they leaped onto the uncut logs and quickly dropped down flat on the long, slanted roof next to the barn. With just their ears and eyes peeking over the ridge, they silently waited.

It was not a long wait. Out of the field behind the kitchen-garden fence, a large female raccoon poked her nose. Her beady eyes looked around carefully through the rails and then she came under the gate followed by her two cubs. All three slowly walked on the grass beside the garden and headed toward the barn.

Pounce started to his feet, but Catcher hissed at him.

"Hiss, down. Hiss, down."

Pounce dropped where he was as Catcher whispered very low to him. "This is bad, Pounce. Wally's in town and there are new kittens in the barn. The chickens were let out to peck for bugs in the field. A raccoon can kill them or kill a cat. This is bad. This is really bad."

Both cats flattened themselves on the woodshed roof. Tension held their fur erect. Barely breathing, their eyes narrowed, they stared without moving and watched the raccoons slowly make their way towards them.

CHAPTER 5

Bull Routs Coons

The big raccoon waddled across the lawn by the garden without attempting to climb the garden fence. She raised her head and swung it from side to side, stopping once in a while for her cubs to catch up. All three sniffed every interesting spot and even turned over a few stones as they came closer.

At the edge of the walk leading to the house, something caught the mother raccoon's attention. She began sniffing and digging in the dirt of the large crockery flowerpot resting on its base. Her leaning weight suddenly tipped the pot over with a heavy thump. Mama coon played in the overturned dirt a moment longer, dug out a couple of flower bulbs, and then seemed to lose interest.

Pounce started to whisper.

"Hush," Catcher whispered back with her nose in Pounce's ear. "I'll explain everything later," her faint voice continued as the cats trembled on the woodshed roof.

How does this strange looking creature know that Wally is not home? Pounce wondered, his little cat heart beating as fast as it had when he fled from the coyote.

The raccoons crossed the wide driveway and open space between the house and the barn as the cats slunk even lower behind the woodshed ridge. Catcher whispered again so low that Pounce almost missed it. "Oh, no. The kittens. She's heading toward the barn."

BANG! SLAM! The noise startled both the raccoons and the cats. It came from the bullpen as the young bull dragged his water tub around. CRASH! WHAM! The short length of rope Matthew had left dangling from the bull's halter had caught under a small split in the rolled metal edge of the tub. Every time Brawny raised his head, he jerked the tub up. The uproar continued accompanied by bull snorts and bellows. "Mauuh! Mauuh!"

More crashing, clanking noises came from the south side of the barn as the bull yanked his tub around inside the pen. CRACK! Brawny crashed through the wooden side of his enclosure. Around the barn he bolted, bellowing and stepping on and kicking the galvanized tub as it swung wildly on his halter rope. Every leap meant another blow from the tub to his chest and legs accompanied by more snorts and bellows.

The raccoons stood on their hind legs and froze as this bull and tub apparition rushed toward them while the cats, also frozen in fear, cowered on the woodshed roof.

All at once the bull spied the coons and slid to a stop, spraying the air with gravel and clouds of dust. He pawed the ground with his front hooves, lowered his head and glared at the raccoons. Then he aimed his small lyre-shaped horns at what he perceived to be his newest threat. His eyes rolled white with rage and he bellowed again as he charged headlong at the raccoons who, in a rare moment of coon sanity, began running for their lives.

The raccoons ran, the young bull pursued, and the tub, like some new kind of giant musical instrument, played a battle song that could have been called *Bang the Bull and Ground*. Across the driveway, over the lawn and alongside the garden they careened, the bull and the tub taking out the garden fence in one noisy swoosh. Wire and posts flew everywhere. The racket was deafening but also exhilarating to the cats standing to watch the running coons and the charging bull.

"Yowl! Yowl!" They added their loud approval to the scene

and jumped from the woodshed to follow the action. "Come on, Pounce. Faster. Let's see if the bull catches them."

They pelted across the lawn, past the garden, into the pasture, and started down the slight hill toward the river. But before they got there they heard the squeal of the horses. "Heee! Wheee!" Up from the deep grass by the river charged the horses, both of them bucking and kicking and whinnying as they came. Clods of dirt and field grass torn loose by their pounding hooves flew into the air.

Chickens pecking in the field squawked and ran every which way. Feathers flew and a couple of the smaller hens went air borne as they looked for a safe roost. Two little gray hens plopped down on the lowest branch of a pasture tree just as Catcher and Pounce reached its foot, exciting them even more. Just then the horses thundered by and the two cats leaped into the tree. They scrambled past the frightened, squawking hens and clawed their way up into the tree's canopy. From this new perch high above the ground the cats swirled around, not sure which way to look.

The cows and the young steers came bellowing up out of the hollow from among the cottonwoods at the north end of the pasture. In every direction the sounds, sights, and excitement continued as the bawling bull and his banging tub seemed to be orchestrating this unrehearsed animal concert. The cats continued to swing their heads back and forth from the bucking horses to the bawling bovines to the bull and tub as they hung on to their branches in the tree. It was a totally enthralling rodeo, a noisy sight with equines bucking and whinnying and bovines kicking and bawling as they all charged around the river pasture looking to escape from the one bull band and his loud tub drum.

The coons were nowhere to be seen, having escaped somewhere along the river, yet the steers, cows, and horses continued to race through the very large pasture. Reaching the fence by the garden, they leaped through the opening the bull had broken in the fence with the young steers in the lead, followed by the cows being driven and herded by the riderless horses. In seconds the herd cleared the path by the downed garden fence and bounded into the main yard by the barn. Circling the yard, the steers bolted through the fence and headed back to their cottonwood grove but the horses and cows stayed behind, having found something more interesting closer to home.

By this time Catcher was laughing so hard she nearly lost her grip on her branch. Her companion breathed in gasps and realized that maybe he wasn't as healed as he had thought. His side hurt and he needed a lot more hair on his body before running through pasture brush and up into trees, but he was laughing too. All of his fear had fled with the raccoons and this was more fun than he'd had in a long time.

Down by the river everything finally grew quiet. The bellowing from the bull and the banging of the tub stopped. The mottled flock of chickens began calmly pecking at all the bugs stirred up by the ruckus, and the little gray hens dropped from their branch to the ground and began pecking where they landed, their adventure totally forgotten.

It also was quiet up in the yard. The horses nosed their way into a fresh bale of hay by the barn and began munching greedily. The cows spread themselves out and began eating the spring lawn by the house, cutting up the grass with their hoofs and burying their fat noses deep into Bonny's carefully tended front yard. They were munching up every tasty thing Bonny cherished. The fresh shoots from the flower bulbs were the first to go along with most of the bulbs. All fear of the raccoons, the bull, and the tub drum was forgotten.

"Well, Catcher. I guess I've been introduced to the bull, the horses, and the cows. Do you have something special planned when I meet the pig?" Pounce was still panting a bit but smiling.

"Oh, Pounce. What a day. What a wild, funny day. I'll take

you for proper introductions when things are quiet around here. Ha, ha, ha." Catcher couldn't stop laughing. "I'm so glad Brawny broke out. What a sight, a bull beating a tub." She hooted with joy. "Me-ow-ee! Like a drummer in a parade, you know?"

Pounce was still laughing too, but the question piqued his interest. "No. I don't know," he answered slowly. "What's a parade?"

"It's this way, Pounce. Humans like parades. They dress themselves up and then they dress up their animals and their cars and their trucks real fancy like. Some of them walk down the street beating a big round tub called a drum that has a bottom and a top. They beat it with sticks and everyone claps. It's loud and obnoxious. Still, humans seem to like obnoxious things."

Pounce liked her use of the word obnoxious and planned on learning to use it as soon as he found a good place for it. He said it over and over as Catcher talked and grinned as he silently formed it without opening his mouth. It made the roof of his mouth tickle. *Obnoxious. Obnoxious. Where will I put you, Obnoxious?*

"The noise makes the horses prance and snort just like Matthew's horses did. Dogs seems to enjoy it too and get real excited when their humans have parades."

Pounce came back from his inward musings to ask, "But why? Why do they have parades?"

"I don't know, but I think men just naturally like to show off. My old owner put his cats in cages in the back of a truck one time in a parade. It was awful. The drums were loud and the noise hurt my ears. When we stopped some people came and put their fingers in the cages trying to touch us. I was so frightened. Then we moved on and my owner pulled me out, lifted me high overhead and stretched me out in the air for people to see my pretty coat. A couple of other humans had signs. They shouted out to the crowd as we drove by to come to the cat show. I never was so terrified in my life."

This last was spoken quietly and Pounce had to listen carefully to hear what Catcher said. He leaned forward and touched her nose, acknowledging that he understood. Of course, he didn't understand, nor did he know what she had been through and Catcher knew it. But the gesture touched her, and she wrinkled her eyes at him in a cat smile.

The two cats backed down out of the tree and started toward the house and barn. Pounce lifted his feet extra high looking for soft places to put them and also watching to avoid any more stickers and pointy things in the brush. He felt sore all over his body from the wild dash they'd taken.

Blackie sat in the back door of the barn as they approached. After Catcher greeted her, Blackie even let Pounce greet her with a nose touch. The three cats turned to walk back into the depths of the barn.

"Oh, Blackie, I was so frightened for your kittens," Catcher murmured.

"Yeah, girl. Me too. I would of fought for 'um if I coulda." She coughed a bit from the barn dust and continued. "I was just starting to grab one and head up into the loft when the Yellow Boys came in the back door. They's a mess and I'm not drawn to 'um much, but you gotta hand it to 'um for they walked right up and the big 'un said to me, 'Little missus, we be right here. Coon-face will have her a time pickin' on all three of us. Her babies ain't big 'nough to help her much and us cats will mop up on that old nasty thing.'"

Pounce stopped in the aisle in amazement. *The Yellow Boys were willing to fight for a wild cat and her kittens? Mama kitty, those scruffy cats must have hearts after all!* He walked faster to catch up to the girls as they talked. Suddenly he saw Catcher reach over and give Blackie a quick lick on the ear. The feral cat turned and looked into Catcher's face intently before continuing to walk.

"Yeah, Catch girl. Yeah, I know. That was close."

When they reached the kitten hideout, the Yellow boys were lounging on top of a nearby straw bale. Big Yellow called down. "Hey, house puss. You gonna spend your life in a tree?"

"Yeah! Youse was up in a tree I saw. I saw," Little Yellow added.

Pounce dropped down on the barn floor and the girls gracefully leaped up on the bales.

"'Tanks, guys." Blackie nodded toward the Yellow Boys and then disappeared down the hole to be with her kittens.

Catcher looked at the yellow cats and answered for Pounce. "I was in the tree too, fellows, and was really glad it was there when we needed it."

Pounce was tired and also happy in a new sort of way. This fright had ended well for the cats and he was glad he didn't have to face it alone. A thought crossed his mind. *It's funny, the teasing and mocking of the Yellow Boys doesn't bother me now.* Then he spoke in a friendly and slow fashion.

"It's all new to me, boys. Farm life, tame animals, wild animals, kittens, *and* yellow cats." Pounce chuckled as he spoke and looked at the two toughies. They had, in fact, turned out to be pussycats when it came to kittens.

Catcher gave her girlie giggle and lay down with her face looking down into the kitten hole. She had a pleasant, relaxed look on her face as she watched the kittens nurse.

"So cute," she whispered down to Blackie. "So cute."

"You fellows called anything but Yellow Boys? I mean; do you have names?"

Pounce looked from one yellow whiskered face to the other and waited.

"Ah, well," the larger of the two yellow cats began and then, putting his paw on his companion, he instantly coaxed the smaller cat into a tussle in the straw. Rolling and biting and kicking each other, they finally rolled off the bale and fell onto the barn floor. Landing on their feet but still worked up from the excitement of the day, they took off running here and there, chasing each other until they disappeared somewhere else in the barn.

Catcher answered the question for Pounce. "They don't like

their names, Pounce, and prefer to be known as a pair. They are brothers, you know."

"I know but ..." his voice trailed off as Catcher interrupted him.

"Yes, I know what you mean. It's nice to have your own identity, and not always to be known by the family you belong to, or the group you hang out with. The Yellow Boys are adult cats, sort of, but they haven't grown up very much. I think I can help them but we'll see."

"Are you going to tell me their names?" Pounce pushed for the information.

Catcher looked at him and giggled. "You don't give up quickly, do you?"

"Nope. I'm one deter-minted pussycat."

"You mean *determined*," she corrected. "And the answer is, the Yellow Boys were poorly named by the boy on the farm where they lived; that is, before they came here to be our barn cats. They were given rude names that they don't deserve. Every animal here doesn't need to know what those names were. Sometimes, keeping silent is kinder. Don't you think so?"

Before Pounce could think so or answer her, the cats heard the pickup truck coming up the driveway. They forgot their talk and scampered out of the storeroom hall to the main aisle and out to the front barn door.

Wally was out of the truck first and he woofed at Matthew to hurry up. Matthew saw that the bullpen was broken and empty, the water tub was gone, and the garden fence was down. He saw the horses calmly eating hay from a pawed open bale alongside the barn and he ignored them. All but one of the cows had wondered back into the pasture, but were grazing close by the downed fence. The oldest cow was still munching the lawn. Matthew took it all in.

"Go to the house, Bonny, and stay inside until I return."

"Matthew?" There was concern in Bonny's voice.

"Do as I say, honey. Back in the truck, Wall." Wally sprang up into the back of the truck while Matthew sprinted for the house. For a big man he could move fast. He reached inside the door and grabbed his rifle where it hung above the coat wall pegs. He was into the pickup and driving back out before Bonny got into the house.

"Pounce?" The fright in Bonny's voice carried across the yard, and the senior cow on the lawn even raised her head for a moment.

"I have to go in now, Catcher. Tomorrow?" He leaned over and gave Catcher a sudden touch with his nose just above one of her beautiful green eyes. Then he turned and trotted toward the house and was caught up by Bonny.

"Oh, kitty. What happened here? You all right?" Bonny lifted Pounce high and examined him before carrying him into the house on her shoulder. Catcher wistfully watched after them from the barn and Pounce read the longing in her eyes before the house door shut on them. A moment later the door reopened and Bonny called again. "Catcher? Come here, girl."

Catcher didn't waste a minute but sped across the driveway and was up in Bonny's arms to be crooned over and petted. She remained in the house with Pounce until she was checked for injuries, given a special treat, and put back outside. It was a delicious end to her day.

Matthew drove his pickup out of his yard as though heading back to town and then took the first left off the main road onto a smaller dirt road that wound down to the river.

Only one gate would need to be opened en route, and it saved him from checking the large pasture on foot. After passing through that gate, he noted that the south side of the steer pen by the cottonwood trees was broken down.

Ah. Another fence to mend. How many more? The steers were

grazing peacefully nearby. It was puzzling that all his big animals seemed to be fine, though in the wrong places. *Now, where is my bull?* His heart was racing for he feared that wolves had once again left the mountains and come down into the farmlands. *I know there is a cougar here somewhere, but Lord, help us,* he thought, *wolves ain't been here for years.*

The pounding in his chest was so loud he felt it in his ears by the time he arrived at the river. Skidding the truck on the gravel that ended close to one of the rocky outcroppings near the water, he suddenly stopped and stared straight ahead. Before he could exit the truck, Wally leaped from the back and started barking at the scene. Matthew pounded on the steering wheel and started laughing so hard it made him cough.

The bull stood in the river facing the truck. He was calmly eating the grass that grew on the bank. The galvanized tub appeared smashed and flattened pretty good, but it floated in the water still attached to the bull's halter rope. When the young bull moved, the tub bumped against his legs and side, but he had become accustomed to it and was ignoring it.

"Quiet, Wall," Matthew shouted from the truck. "Brawny seems to be breakin' himself in. No barkin' now, boy. Let's see if this big fellow can be led out of there."

Matthew got out of the pickup slowly and started walking toward his bull, still chuckling, but watching carefully. He didn't have anything in his hand and he wondered if he should pick up a stick in case Brawny opened up and charged. Thinking better of it, he just started talking softly to the bull.

"Hey, boy. Been out strollin' around? I see you took your water tub with you for the walk. Never know when a big fellow like you will get thirsty. Didn't know you were a-comin' to the river, I'll bet."

When he reached the water, Matthew bent over and began to rub the bull between his eyes. He wondered at the calmness of the bull for the river was noisy and its swift current plunged over and slammed into thousands of rocks. Yet where the bull stood was one of Matthew's favorite fishing spots with deep water and a slow moving pool created by the placement of the rocks.

"Ha, scared my trout away, I bet. Didn't you?"

"Huuh. Huuh," Brawny responded. He was quiet and happy to stand in the water and eat grass and now here was the man who gave him buckets of grain too. Life was good. "Huuh."

Matthew continued to talk softly while he studied the tub and halter hookup. The end of the rope was tightly wedged into the crushed edge of the tub so he finally decided to cut it loose with his pocketknife. He began sawing at the halter rope just above the tub that was held by the current close to the bull's shoulder. Matthew worked slowly lest he accidently prick his bull with his knife tip.

"That's a good bull, Brawny. I'll have your head free in a moment." The last strand of rope separated, the bull jerked his head up, the rope slipped out of Matthew's fingers, and the current bumped the tub once more against the bull's side. No explosion took place. Brawny stood still, only turning his body sideways a bit as the tub passed behind him and slipped down steam, disappearing in the distance.

"Ah, bully! I shoulda kept a better hold on that severed end. Now there's a find for someone down river. Hey, boy? They'll wonder about it, I'll bet," Matthew chuckled. "Well, let's see. Can you be led, big fella? Do I need Wally to send you home?"

Matthew pulled on the end of the small piece of rope still attached to Brawny's halter. The bull had never worn a nose ring like many bulls do, and Matthew wondered if he'd made a mistake in not having one put on his bull. While he was still thinking, Brawny slowly moved his bulk up and out of the water following the tug on his head.

"So far, my boy. So far, that's good." Matthew kept up a low patter of speech to help calm the bull, but Brawny seemed perfectly calm whether Matthew was talking or not. When they gained level ground and the bull kept moving, Matthew decided to keep walking and hoped the bull would too.

"Wall. Go round." The big collie slowly circled the bull and took up his position about twenty feet behind them while Matthew turned his back on Brawny and walked confidently across the large pasture. They passed under the tree where the cats had watched the rodeo, then reached the fence line and stepped through the broken railings next to the garden. The bull stepped smartly along behind the man's legs. He was so close that Matthew could feel the bull's breath on his hand, the halter rope was that short. Brawny gave a low snort of greeting to the younger cows grazing next to the fence line when they passed, but followed Matthew as docile as a well-trained pony.

Along the downed garden fence and alongside the torn-up lawn in front of the house they walked, and when they gained the gravel driveway to the barn, Matthew only shook his head at his senior cow. She ignored the man and bull and continued to methodically dine on the lawn. Finally, they walked down the driveway to the barn's east side and stepped over the lowest broken rail into the bullpen. Brawny followed him step for step.

"My word, bull. Am I happy with you or what?" Once in the pen, Matthew walked the bull in a couple of circles to see if he would still follow. He did. It was done. Brawny had been trained to lead by a washtub and a halter rope.

"It will cost some to replace all this, but my, oh my. You, bully boy, lead just fine."

Matthew grabbed another rope that was hanging over the post in the center of the corral and tethered Brawny's halter to it. Then he went to the barn and returned with a bucket holding some grain and another filled with water.

"Good fellow. Gotta get you another tub, but that's in the loft and you gotta wait 'till mornin', he said as he fed the bull and stroked his face. He carefully checked the black hair around Brawny's expressive eyes, ran his hands up and down the bull's ears and studied the animal's black fleshy nose for cuts or gashes. The animal seemed fine. He then threw some big flakes of sweet hay to Brawny.

"Ay, boy. That'll do ya 'till 'morrow, I bet."

He paused to scratch the root of Brawny's tail, then stepped back and carefully eyed his new bull. The animal's legs and belly were wet but his beautiful coat seemed clean and undamaged. His handsome face was marked in black and white, his ears were black, and down the length of his back was a wide white stripe. He never tired of thinking about how these Randall cattle could have black skin under white hair.

Matthew couldn't see any cuts, but he ran his hands down the bull's mostly dark sides while Brawny had his head in the grain pail. *What funny and beautiful things they are,* he mused. "Good boy. Good boy, old bully bull. Yeah!"

Matthew crossed the bullpen and walked back over the broken rails and then turned into the pasture by the milking parlor door. Opening the door to the barn he said, "Come, Wall. Cows."

Wally moved off to round up the cattle without needing another command while Matthew started his walk back to get his truck in the field. Seeing Bonnie on the porch watching, he called. "It's okay, love. I'll tell you all about it when I get back." She nodded and disappeared inside.

It was dusk and he was already tired. The cows must be milked and the horses put in their stalls for the night. They didn't seem injured but Matthew would check them for scrapes when he bedded them all down for the night. He sighed and kept walking. Sometimes he wondered how long he could keep farming like this. He was getting older. But then something would catch his fancy like the Randall cattle breed had several years earlier.

He had bred his new Randall cows to his aging bull and the offspring were nice, but now he had the young Randall bull with his small curved horns. *Like in a picture book,* he thought. *Ah, the bull.* He forgot his age and went somewhere in his head where he dreamed of the great calves they would raise from this fine Randall bull and those pretty Randall cows.

Matthew could hardly wait. The dream encouraged him. After the mixed breed steers were sold this fall, Brawny and the cows would give him a new start with something he'd dreamed of for years. He had always wanted to raise a few good animals from an endangered American cattle breed.

A stream of thought like that was fulfilling to think along, but that was for tomorrow, and this was today so Matthew returned to the present. He needed to lock the chickens up, put food down for the cats, and fill the pig trough. There was still sweet feed in the back of the truck that needed unloading as well as the groceries that Bonny had purchased. He was suddenly hungry too. Matthew quickened his steps as he went through the break in the fence, passed his young cows, and disappeared into the field for the truck.

The cows moved toward the dog as their full utters swung against their back legs giving them a duck-like waddle.

"Home, girls. Woof. Woof." When the first cow entered the milking room, Wally circled back and firmly told the lawn cow to get her spotted hide into the barn or else. One serious bark was all it took for her to leave the lawn and do as she was told.

In the house, dinner was cooking and smelling up the place with delicious scents.

Pounce talked to Bonny as he walked back and forth by her feet. He told her everything about this exciting day as she boiled potatoes and fried onions and made coffee. Other bowls and plates gave off wonderful smells and Pounce wanted so much to get up and see what was in them. He could hardly contain himself as he kept talking to Bonny. He told her about his hungry stomach, and the raccoons, and being up in a tree, and the bucking horses, and the Yellow Boys, and the kittens, and oh, there was so much to say.

After supper, Pounce purred in Bonny's lap as she pulled the twigs and stickers from his soft and very short coat. Bonnie laughed at her cat, somehow thinking that the noise was because he had missed her that day. She examined his hip and traced her finger over the scar where she had put in the stitches. It had flattened down a lot and she hoped that enough hair would grow to cover the entire area.

Then she studied his feet while he dozed upside down in her lap. He didn't mind when she pulled his toes and ran her fingers between them. It felt so good that he spread his hind toes out even more so she could tickle them, though his pads in places were still somewhat tender. The glass cuts had been very deep and his pads were not quite ready for the events the animals had obviously experienced.

When Pounce finally fell asleep, he slept so deeply that he didn't remember being put in his dresser bed. Nor did he know that he was secretly kissed on his forehead by Bonny when she thought Matthew wasn't watching. But he was kissed, and Matthew, though pretending not to see, did see, and the age creases around his eyes deepened as he chuckled silently, twitching his lips as he always did when his wife delighted him.

What delicious and exciting dreams the kitty had that night. He twitched and jerked and snored and wiggled his whiskers and smiled his pussycat smile and then did it all over again.

CHAPTER **6**

Skin and Hair

Matthew hired the Anderson brothers to plow a special patch of ground in the east side pasture for more corn. Some would be for the pigs, but the real reason for the extra corn was Bonny urging him to get her more dry ears to sell in the fall.

Though he didn't understand why the women wanted to decorate with dry ears of corn, he knew Bonny and her friends were excited about the beautiful decorations they would make. Matthew even had to purchase some fancy seeds for his wife's "special" rows but, even while grumbling, deep down he was always happy to please Bonny.

This new corn patch was fairly near the house and surrounded by the hay fields. The Anderson brothers finished the corn patch and then aerated the rest of the pasture. The thousands of tiny holes they drilled in the ground would let more air and moisture get to the roots. Finally they spread a mixture of grass seeds and cured manure to help the pasture produce the best blend of feed for Matthew's cows and horses the following winter. During the summer months, the Larsen animals had many acres to graze on close to the river and those pastures grew lushly most of the year, but the land on the east side needed extra attention.

Matthew dug up Bonny's garden by the house and within several days Pounce was walking the rows of freshly dug earth in the garden while Bonny planted seeds.

"This is not a kitty box, Pounce. Don't you dare," Bonny scolded and watched him closely. But Pounce merely sniffed the freshly dug earth and followed Bonny closely. She began to cover the seeds quickly because he took a special interest in the larger ones, especially beans. They looked liked little dark beetles and he wanted to bat them around.

While Bonny planted and Pounce considered everything that was going on, Matthew busied himself with putting in new garden posts and raising animal-proof wire around the garden. After several days of this activity, Pounce found himself outside the garden with the tall wire gate shut in his face.

"You'll get used to it, Pounce," Catcher told him. "It's one of those places where you must never go when the gate is closed. We are not allowed to be cats in the garden, if you know what I mean."

One late spring morning, when the air was warm and long wispy clouds streaked the brilliant blue sky, Catcher took Pounce to meet the cows and horses. "It's important to be friends with the big horses, Pounce. I think they may be Matthew's favorite animals on the farm except for Wally. But let's go meet the cows first."

Pounce nodded without understanding. *Why was it important to like big animals?* He was puzzled yet strolled alongside Catcher, willing to go anywhere she led. They approached the cows in the milk barn first. Up close they appeared even bigger which made Pounce feel very small.

The bovines were standing quietly in their stanchions waiting to be milked. Pounce immediately leaped to a stall rail high off the floor and nowhere near their hooves, but Catcher walked confidently among the cows, waving her tail in greeting and speaking softly to them.

The cows' coats were of medium length slick hair and were a lot like Pounce's own coat. The youngest among them had the most beautiful black and white face. She had long, black eyelashes and a mixture of swirling black and white hairs that gave her face a peppered look. She looked like she was wearing a little black cap on the top of her head. Her nose was black and so were her ears. Her body was covered with both large black spots and numerous small ones except for the middle of her back. It was white all down her back.

She glanced up at Pounce from time to time as Pounce sat on the rail and stared down at her. He was completely entranced by her pretty coat and beautiful face. He finally looked away from her chewing face, an action he didn't think very pretty, and stared at her feet. The two front legs were black up to her knees, and her rear legs were white.

Wow! Pounce thought. *She looks like some of my brothers and sisters.* He glanced down at his own legs in comparison and was amazed at how her patterned hide reminded him of his family. *Wow!* He said it again to himself. *Except for the species, we could be related.* Pounce hummed with delight at his own humor.

The three cows continued to pull and chew hay as Catcher introduced Missy to Pounce up on his stall railing perch. "This pretty lady you are looking at is Missy and she is the youngest of the Randall cattle."

Missy looked up at Pounce and bawled with her mouth full. A large bite of hay fell out onto the barn floor. The whole thing was startling and a bit loud. Pounce tensed and he looked over at Catcher who stood on the floor near the cow that had eaten most of the lawn. He had no idea what Missy said or even if she was really saying anything. Before he could ask, the largest cow cleared her throat and mooed almost directly in Catcher's face. Catcher closed her eyes, and Pounce sensed that cow breath was not Catcher's favorite fragrance. However, Catcher politely said nothing and introduced the mooing bovine.

"And this matron is Melody. She was named for the beautiful bell-like tones she makes while mooing and for this bell she wears. Pounce, look at this bell."

How could I miss it? He didn't speak the thought, but looked at the object that hung on a leather strap from Melody's neck. The bell was brass and, every time Melody moved, it rang. He had to admit it was a pleasant sound, though a bit loud for cat ears. The bell reminded Pounce of the horse bells on long leather straps "Mom" had had hanging in her kitchen and had sometimes rung as she passed them.

Melody's coat was red and white. Her sides were mostly dark red and she also had white hair growing down the middle of her back just like Missy. Her legs were dark red and her face was mostly white set off by a nice pair of upright curved horns. Pounce was fascinated by the color of all the cows.

"Pounce, did you know that Melody is able to walk so softly her bell won't ring? Bonny calls her a bell cow because she wears the bell and the other cows follow her. That is, most of the time." Catcher giggled, thinking of Melody on the lawn and the others in the field when Matthew and Bonnie had returned home.

"Bonny bought the bell at a farmer's market for Matthew to put on the first Randall cow he bought. But you watch. Matthew will have it off Melody and hanging up in the barn yet. He doesn't care for the bell but he does care for Bonny."

Catcher giggled her happy little sound, and Pounce grinned back at her. Her giggles and laugher were more pleasant and tinkling than the cowbell, and certainly easier on his ears.

"Melody is one smart cow. She is the mother of Marigold, but not of Missy."

Pounce swung his head and carefully tried to remember it all. Yes, he could see that the light colored cow Marigold looked just like the red Melody cow, but the black and white Missy was not like either of them.

"Matthew calls Marigold his red roan and thinks she would be a winner in a cow show. Isn't she beautiful?" Before Pounce could say yes, Catcher went on, "Do you know what he says these close speckled marks are called?"

"Spots?"

"Yes, of course, but he told Bonny that these cows were *brockled*, and that means sort of roan-like."

"Ha! That's funny. What kind of word is *brockled*, or *roan* for that matter?"

"I don't know. But I think people use both words to mean bits of color on a white background."

"They should say speckled or spotted, and then everyone would know what they mean."

"Well, Pounce, people use lots of words cats don't understand and I expect that lots of other people don't understand them either."

At that, both cats laughed and the cows mooed as though they were laughing too.

Catcher moved over to Marigold and Pounce had to agree that she was very pretty and her shiny red coat was so light in places it looked like it had yellow in it. *Like the yellow boys*, Pounce thought. Hers was the lightest coat of all the cows.

Pounce remembered how, on the bull and coon day, he had seen the sun glinting off Marigold's sides as she ran by. Her horns were shorter than Melody's, not curled upward as much and were a creamy color. Marigold also had a wide white line of hair growing down the full length of her back and her face was mostly white. She made him think of his mama who had large round golden eyes in a white face. *I must miss my family. I am looking at huge cows and thinking of tiny cats.* He hummed inwardly again and then laughed out loud.

"I get it! Didn't you tell me once that some people call them Randall cattle, and others call them Randall Lineback cattle? They all got a line down their backs. I get it!" He was pleased with himself and sat up a bit straighter and Catcher tittered in amusement before quietly correcting him.

"*Have.* All of them *have* a line down their backs."

Pounce didn't miss the point and shot right back. "That's what I said. They all have got a line down their backs."

Catcher decided to ignore Pounce's humor and continue her lesson. "Missy is pretty young but had her first calf this spring. It's that pretty little black and white one in the large stall down there. See? Stand up on your hind legs, Pounce, and you will see. There, with the large red and white calves. Of course, all three calves were born out in the field this spring."

Pounce stood and, balancing himself on the top rail, peered down the aisle of the milk barn and into the main barn toward the stall where the bawling calves were protesting not being with their mothers.

"These are real tough cattle, Pounce. While you were lying around in the house healing up, these ladies were having babies outside in the cold weather. Aren't they indeed strong and lovely ladies?" This last was said with such smiling eyes and affection that all three cows set up a low mooing in return.

"Missy came to the farm recently and she is such a dear." Catcher smiled at the youngest cow and got a long moo in her face for the effort. "Marigold has had two calves. One is a spotted yearling steer penned with Melody's last year's calf. They have a lot of red color on them. They are penned with the black steers in the north corner of the big pasture by the water. The black ones are from the cattle Matthew had before these lovelies arrived. They are two years old now, and I heard Matthew say they were sold. So I guess all the steers will be leaving soon."

Pounce was beginning to feel overwhelmed by all the information, but Catcher tripped back and forth between the cows, rubbing against their legs, completely at home with everything about the cows.

"Look here, Pounce. It's hard to tell because the cows still have a bit of their winter coats. But under this good thick hair, even where the hair is white, they often have some black skin. Isn't that funny? You have white skin under your black coat. See? Where you are shaved."

Pounce was suddenly a little embarrassed, but tried not to show it.

"Matthew says that it's strange these cows can have lots of black skin with white hair growing out of it. Bonny said that it is not strange for even people with dark skin can grow white hair on their heads when they are old. Remember what you asked about the speckled kitten? See! We're all the same, no matter what color of skin we have."

Pounce liked this bit of information. It was small enough for him to remember, and how could he forget that white hair could grow out of black skin as easily as black hair could grow out of white skin?

He began to forget the size of the cows and his still mostly short coat and hummed to himself a quick little skin and hair song. *Skin and hair, it is there, everywhere we see. It's on him. It's on her. It's on you and me.* But, before he could finish his composing and break out in song, Catcher interrupted his mental world.

"Well, ladies. This cat is Pounce. See how his coat will look when it grows out. It is much like your coats. Isn't that funny?"

Catcher smiled and the cows mooed again, but Pounce couldn't understand a thing they said. They just stood in their places chewing as Matthew washed their utters in preparation for milking and the small black and white calf and the two large red calves kept up their bawling in their stall. Between the noisy calves and the mooing cows, Pounce was confused. Their sounds didn't make sense to him. It seemed to be one word, "Moo-owe. Moo-owe." Pounce cocked his head and listened again. "Are they trying to say move over?"

Catcher saw his puzzled look and laughed. "It's a simple language and you can get it if you listen hard. They are really quite nice and they like cats. Jump down here and get a squirt of milk when Matthew begins milking. It's delicious."

Pounce held back and looked again at their size. He tried to understand them, but still, all he heard was noise and it was loud in his little cat ears. Catcher, however, seemed to be having a regular talk with the cows.

"My friends, thank you for the warm milk. It's very good today. Did you get into the clover patch yesterday down by the willows? " As Catcher thanked the cows, she wove between their legs, rubbing her head on each cow, purring loudly and looking up directly into their faces.

"Moo-owe."

"I thought so. Well done. Well done. How does the lawn compare to field grass? Better?"

"Moo-owe."

"I thought it might."

"Moo-owe."

"No, you won't be allowed to eat lawn again."

"Moo-owe."

"Well, maybe. You could be right. The humans may grow it to eat themselves though I've never seen them eat the lawn after they cut it. I think they put the cuttings over in the garden."

"Moo-ove."

"Well, that's right. It does seem wasteful I'm sure, to a cow."

Pounce laughed at that but Catcher gave him a strong glance. It all seemed so strange to Pounce and especially Catcher's glance, so he finally spoke up, "If cats were meant to talk to cows, I would understand them."

"Shush, Pounce. Don't be rude to them. They can understand you, even if you can't understand them. If we can't understand someone, it's easy to think that they are not smart. But," she smiled up at the listening cows, "actually, they are very smart." All the cows began mooing loudly again. "Pounce, your city ears are not trained to hear country sounds yet. Just watch and listen. Now, hop down here. This warm milk is incredible."

Looking again at the cows, Catcher worked damage control. "He doesn't mean any harm, ladies. He was raised in a city house and has never been in the country before."

The cows nodded and kept chewing as Pounce hopped down and carefully moved closer to Matthew's side, and then waited.

Matthew finally noticed him. "Haw, cat! Have a bit of this," he said and pointed the teat at Pounce. The next thing Pounce knew the warmest, most delicious milk he had ever tasted wet his face and whiskers. Matthew laughed as Pounce stood up on his hind legs in an attempt to catch the next stream. Another arc of milk came his way and this time Pounce had his mouth open, at least part of the time. It was a wonderful treat and Catcher was right. Warm milk straight out of the teat was grand.

Pounce could see that Matthew was content and quiet while milking. He had his big head pushed into the side of Melody and the rhythm of the milk hitting the sides of the pail was pleasant to listen to.

The cows had stopped talking and gone back to munching their hay. Their long tails switched back and forth. The only sounds were those of the cats walking up and down mewing for another squirt of warm milk and the constant bawling of the calves. Pounce walked down to where the calves were penned and began watching them though the stall rails. He had to agree with Catcher. They were pretty, especially the little black and white one.

"They will be sold when they are a bit larger as they can't be kept here on the farm with Brawny since they are bull calves," Catcher said as she walked up behind him.

Pounce wondered why, but he didn't ask.

"I heard Matthew tell Bonny he really likes that little black and white bull calf." Catcher paused and, looking away, added,

"Bonny likes black and white critters too and I suppose that's why you are her favorite right now." Catcher laughed as Pounce turned wide eyes toward her. "I'm just teasing, Pounce, color is not as important as confirmation."

"Confirmation?"

"That means the over-all shape of an animal has to look right. It's how the people will know that the animals are related, like the Morgan horses, for instance. Anyone who looks at them can tell they are not racehorses. Cattle are like that too. The same family of cows will be similar to each other."

"Oh, I see. Like all of us cats look like cats?"

"Well, not quite. There are pure breeds and ..."

"Ha. Gotcha! You mean and other cats like me?"

Catcher saw that he was teasing her right back and wrinkled her nose at him before going on. "Missy's baby is purebred Randall, and the other calves are only half Randall. Matthew hopes some farmers will want them for bulls on their farms when they grow up. Matthew will feed them real well all summer and, for a while yet, he will let them nurse on their mamas."

"That's nice."

"Did you know that Bonny and Matthew used to sell milk? A big, round truck used to come here and take away the milk but it doesn't anymore since Matthew sold his other cows. The pig gets a lot of milk now, Bonny gives some of it away, and she says she will have a new use for extra milk soon."

Pounce didn't know one vehicle from another. Up until now, he had been hidden away in the house in his dresser drawer, or sleeping on the soft cushions under the window. But he nodded as though he understood.

"Matthew says he's too old to start milking a herd again although he never had a big herd, only about a dozen cows." Catcher was in some kind of bliss as she talked. It was obvious that she loved the farm and everything about it. Pounce could hardly take his eyes from her pretty face as she rambled on and on.

"Do you see those round machines over there and the hoses and such?"

Pounce nodded, but he didn't turn his head to look. His eyes were fastened on Catcher's animated whiskers and blinking eyes.

"Those are milking machines, and Matthew said he will use the machines again, but for now he is just enjoying his beautiful cows."

Pounce nodded again, but he wasn't sure what she was talking about.

"Bonny and a couple of her friends are planning to make cheese out of this good milk. They have to get some special tubs and things put into the milk storage room. I'm not sure what cheese is, yet it sounds lovely."

Pounce remembered cheese. His "Mom" used to feed him little bits of white and yellow cheese from her fingers. He started to tell Catcher how good cheese tasted but she was babbling along happily. So Pounce just sat near her and washed his milky whiskers while trying to take it all in.

"Matthew was disappointed when the ladies had bull calves and not heifers. Did you notice all that white hair down their backs?"

"Yes. I did. Right away. I wish you could have met my bothers and sisters. They were real pretty like that too, but they didn't have white hair down the middle of their backs."

"I'm sure they were pretty, Pounce, I'm sure they were. But these Randall cows are special heirloom cattle."

"What's that mean?"

"I'm not real sure. Matthew talks to the other farmers who visit, and they say these come from a very old family of cows that are real old–fashioned, American cows. Not many of them are alive so Matthew is raising them here to help save the family line."

"What a fine thing to do. Matthew must really like cows."

"Well, he does like cows, but not just any kind. He sold his other cows so he could help save this breed for he doesn't want them to become extinct. People with great big farms have lost interest in them. But Matthew says it will be important in the future for people to save things now that are good. You know, like pure strains of everything like cattle and chickens and pigs and horses and plants and, well, lots of living things."

"What's a future?"

"Oh, Pounce. It means tomorrow. Oh, you!"

Catcher caught the twinkle in his eyes and understood that he was teasing her again.

She giggled and said, "Oh, you. I guess I have been playing the teacher too long today, haven't I?"

"No, I love it. It's nice to see how interested you are in everything around here. I like it, Catcher. And I like hearing about pure stuff. Like you."

"I'm a cat. Any cat can catch a mouse, purebred or not. Sure, people want to see pure breeds of cats, yet good farm animals are even more important because they are necessary for people. I heard the men talk about how healthy these Randall cattle are and useful for everything. The other men told Matthew to stop giving his cows and the bull so much grain. They don't need it like other kinds of cattle. They thrive on good pasture grass. So Matthew is cutting back some, but he does like to spoil them. Bonny said Vermont even named the Randall breed as the state breed of cattle."

"Really? What's a state?" Pounce asked seriously.

"What's a state? States are places we live in this country. They are bigger than these farms and the city you came from and anything else you've seen. It's how the country is divided up. But come, Pounce. For now, states can wait! You've got to meet the horses."

"Bye, ladies," she called back as they trotted away from Matthew and the cows.

CHAPTER 7

Hooves and Paws

Large boulders, millions of rounded rocks, and countless tons of gravel paved the bed of Rocky River and its sides. Except where the pastures rose and thrust overhanging banks out over the water, it was a very rocky river. The fast rushing water bounced and sprayed its way among and over the rocks with an almost deafening roar. Pounce flattened his ears in response as they drew near and forgot that he wanted to ask Catcher why some cattle were called steers and some were called bulls.

On one of the higher, overhanging banks both horses were grazing close together. They seemed awfully big to little Pounce, even bigger than when he had watched them tear around the pasture during the bull and raccoon event. Pounce was not sure he wanted to get close.

"Those feet," he said out loud. "Look at the size of those feet."

"Hooves, Pounce, they are called hooves. Horses and cows have hooves. Cats and dogs have paws. Pigs and chickens and people have feet."

"But how do you know what to call them? I saw the pig in her pen when we walked by and she has hard, split hooves like a cow. How come they call them feet and not hooves?"

Catcher automatically corrected him. "Pounce, you should not say 'how come.' Say, 'Why do they,' etc."

"Okay. Why do they, etc!"

"Okay, funny cat. The funny ones are the people. I heard a neighbor woman talk to Bonny about how to make pickled pigs' feet. She said they were delicious but Bonny wasn't so sure she wanted to eat a pig's foot. That's how I know they are feet and not hooves, even though they do look like small cow hooves."

Catcher let Pounce ponder her words as they sat down a little way from the horses on a higher mound in the pasture. One of the pasture's many broadleaf trees shielded the cats from the brightness of the sun. It was a pleasant place to rest. The breeze was soft and warm and it lightly stirred the leaves and fluffed the cats' coats at the same time. Both cats stretched and began licking themselves. Pounce gave special attention to the pads of his feet. He still felt some tenderness from time to time where the cuts had been deep.

Pounce suddenly chuckled. "That was funny, Catcher. You know, when the cow thought the humans ate the lawn clippings."

"You understood what they said?"

"No, not a word of it. I could tell by your answers. That's how."

"Well, from a cow's point of view, not eating anything green and edible seems wasteful."

At this both cats began to laugh and Pounce finally let out a little sigh. "My old home in the city never prepared me for this." He was relaxed and began to hum to himself. The water flowing over the rocks in the river now seemed to accompany him and he had forgotten the volume of its racket. A minute later his hum came out as a typical Pounce cat song and he flopped over on his back and sang with all his heart.

"Feet and hooves and paws and such, you need to walk about.
Some are pretty and some are not, but all will make you shout.
They're necessary walking tools, needful walking pegs,
Feet and hooves and paws and such on the bottom of our legs,

Oh, feet and hooves and paws and such on the bottom of our legs."

By this time Pounce was waving all four white paws in the air. Catcher sat by his head and looked down into his closed eyes. She studied this city cat and wondered. *He is ignorant of so many things necessary for a cat to know. And yet, there is something deep inside him that erupts from time to time in poetry and song. It is as if he has to sing.* This aspect of her new friend fascinated Catcher more and more.

Where, she wondered, *did he get his song? It is unlike any cat singing I've ever heard. It is more like the singing that human children do.* She remembered her first home and the children in it. They often had sung just like Pounce was doing now. Their songs were about anything and about everything. Adult people didn't sing like that. At least Catcher didn't think so.

Pounce sang his song again and again. His paws gracefully beat out the time as Rock River played cymbals and drums back-up on the stones and boulders in the river behind him.

"Pounce?"

"Huh?" Pounce opened his eyes.

"Oh, Pounce. I like it. How do you make up songs like that?"

He looked up at Catcher. "What?"

"Did you sing about everything when you were a little kitten?"

"I guess so."

"Well, you still do."

"Yup. I guess so. Yup, I dodee, dodee, do!"

Catcher giggled and then laughed out loud. "What makes you start? How do you know to start singing and where do you get the words?"

It was Pounce's turn to chuckle. He sat up and looked at his friend and saw that she was serious. "Catcher, it's like this. When we were little kittens and mewed, mama told us not to just cry. She told us to cry with purpose when we know what we feel. We should know when we're hungry or tired or happy or whatever. She said having a purpose was important for every kitty. It would help us be good learners. She said it didn't matter if our cry was happy or sad, just as long as it was honest."

Pounce paused, remembering. "So, I did what she did. She sang over us and I learned to do what she did. Mama sang when we were eating and playing. She sang when she bathed us and when she scolded us. She always sang. So I copied her and now I sing about most goings-on in my life. I learn faster when I sing."

Catcher listened carefully. "Okay. I think I get it. The words are what you are learning, but where do you get the melody?"

"The melody I make up as I sing. Mama said every living thing has a melody. She said the melody is in our bellies and the words in our heads. So, if I put them together, I sing. When I sing, I hear my own song. It goes back into my ears and drops down again into my belly and I can feel the rightness of things that have been both down in my belly and up in my head. They sort of agree and don't fight, you know?"

Pounce put his head up and down when he said the words *up* and *down* which made Catcher giggle her light, girlish giggle and helped her decide not to correct Pounce for saying *you know*.

"Mama always told us to guard our bellies and to not let any creature bite them. She taught us that good things come out of our bellies when we put good things in. So when what I learn in my head becomes part of my belly, that helps put even more words in my head." Pounce paused, took a deep breath and lowered his voice again. "Mama said it is important to pay attention to what we hear, and to think carefully about things. We must not expect others to do our thinking, just as they cannot do our learning."

Pounce dropped on his side and hummed softly as he licked his front paws before continuing. "Singing helps me understand stuff. You know, to use my cathead? Mama said if I didn't use my cathead, I wouldn't be good for myself or anyone else either. You know?" Pounce was a bit embarrassed when he finished talking so he sucked in his breath and waited.

"My dear friend, what a wonderful mother you must have had."

Pounce nodded vigorously for it was a relief to know that Catcher understood. Then he continued and answered Catcher's unasked question. "My owner, Mom, she sang too, you know. She was very old, but I heard her sing about something every day. I loved to sit in her lap and listen to her sing while she held me. I could feel the sound rumbling around inside her, you know."

Catcher vowed again to teach Pounce to stop saying *you know* unless it fit the sentence. But she held her tongue this time, remembering that she was trying to stop using it herself. Instead, she asked, "What words did she sing?"

"Just like me. Whatever she was thinking about, you know. Sometimes she held a favorite book on her lap and sang the words written in it. Or I'd sit on the kitchen floor and listen to her sing about making tea or something else. It was nice."

"No wonder you sing. You are obeying the simple instructions of your intelligent mother, and doing what your owner did too. I wish," it was Catcher's turn to lower her voice, "I wish I had been taught such things."

Now it was Pounce who could not constrain himself. He leaned forward and patted Catcher right between her ears with one of his paws and then flopped back down in the grass, inviting her to play. His tail twitched in anticipation of a good romp, and Catcher was taken off guard.

"You rascal. Later. For now, come on. Let's go meet the horses. Maybe you'll sing about these fellows."

The horses were quiet and watched the cats approach but they didn't stop grazing. Catcher walked up to within seven feet of the closest horse and sat down. Turning her head away from the horse she began licking her back and side. Then she stood, stretched and calmly walked forward. She looked at the grazing animal several feet away and then, deliberately, walked up to his nearest front leg and slowly rubbed her body against it.

Pounce held his breath. He thought it was an awesome display of bravery, and Catcher had never looked prettier with the sun making her gray and silver coat shimmer. As Catcher rubbed against the leg again, the big horse slowly swung his head sideways and blew his breath on the cat's back. Catcher closed her eyes and raised her head to touch one of his nostrils with her own nose. Then she sat down and spoke quietly, almost in a purr. "Hi, Trump. How's it going?"

A low rumble came from deep inside the horse. "Aw, Catcher. It's good to see you again. I've missed our nightly talks in the barn."

"I know, dear. The wild thing, Blackie, has her kittens now. I'm spending the nights with the Yellow Boys guarding against rats and such. Just till they're a bit older, and it gives Blackie time to go hunting. She likes to hunt at night, being wild and all."

The brown horse's black tail slowly swished against his sides and back legs as he listened. Then he blew his breath over Catcher and inhaled her scent once again. She wrinkled her face in pleasure as his warm exhalation lifted her coat. Then she rubbed the back of her head against his leg in response.

"Something else to talk about now, Trump. This cat is Pounce. He was sewn up by Bonny. A coyote chased him and something hit him and he's been in some sort of fire too. As you can see, his coat's a bit short, and he still moves like his feet hurt him."

"Boo-aah." Trump blew as he lifted his head and put his ears forward, looking intently at Pounce.

"How do you do, sir," Pounce said cautiously.

"Come here, son." The big horse's command came up from somewhere deep in his chest.

Pounce felt his legs turn to straw as they barely held him up. He didn't want anything to do with anyone that big. Yet he obeyed since Catcher was sitting quietly at Trump's feet without showing fear. As he approached, he stiffened his legs and started walking sideways. He could hardly breathe, and he couldn't think. His heart thumped against his ribs with such force, and his coat was so short, that the pounding in his little frame was visible to the horse.

"Heeeeee, haaaaa." Trump laughed and threw his head up and down.

Pounce's stiff walk even got to Catcher, and she fell over on her side giggling.

"Okay, son. Don't be afraid. I've never stepped on a cat yet. Cats, like your Catcher, and me are good friends. She's cleaned many a mouse out of my hay bales and grain bin. Yeah. I like cats. Come here."

Pounce walked straighter and felt better. Not because he had lost his fear of the horse, but because Trump had said, "Your Catcher." Again Pounce held his breath, but this time with the giddiness of his thought. *Can it be? Is it possible? Is Catcher my girl cat?*

All this talk had interested the other horse and he walked over.

"And Spade, this is Pounce," Catcher nodded to the younger horse. She walked over to greet him nose to nose also. Spade dropped his head and put his soft nose under Catcher and gently tipped her over into the grass. Then he blew rollers of his warm breath into her silver belly fur.

"Booo. Boooo," His vibrating lips made Catcher giggle some more.

"Pounce, these big fellows are good friends of mine. I know you will get along just fine."

"How do you do, sir," Pounce repeated to Spade.

"Just fine, little cat. Just fine. Thank you."

Pounce then took his cue from Catcher and greeted both

horses nose to nose. He was surprised at their warm and pleasant breath. A comfortable peace settled down on him as they drew in his scent and then blew warm air all over his head.

Wow, he thought. *Horses are nice. Wow*!

Catcher broke in on Pounce's thoughts as the horses dropped their heads back down into the lush grass and began nipping it off again. "Nice, huh?"

"Yup. Nice." He was still basking in the feeling of that strong current of warm air over his face that also had the pleasant scent of fresh grass.

"Horses like the way we smell too, Pounce, except when we smell of dead mouse. They don't like mouse smell, alive or dead. But when we've walked in the fields, or rolled in their hay and our coats are clean, then they like the way we smell."

"Ah, Catcher. You always smell good to me," Trump answered.

"Pounce, these horses make Matthew proud. He loves them."

Both horses took in a long draft of air and held it for a moment as they listened. Then in a whoosh they exhaled and kept on tearing great mouthfuls of the sweet, spring pasture grass.

"Matthew boosts about these being America's first special kind of horses. They all have a great ancestor horse named Justin Morgan. He was the first Morgan horse. A long time ago horses like these were used to plow fields and work all week. Then on the weekends they took their families by wagon or buggy to shop in town on Saturday and then to church on Sunday. After that they won road races against other farmers and their horses."

"My 'Mom' went to school in a wagon pulled by horses," Pounce said, adding to the lesson.

"Yes, Pounce. Since she was old, no doubt she did. Did her family have Morgan horses?"

"I don't know. I never heard her say what kind of horses they were. But I remember the stories she told her grandson and how wistful she became in telling them. She must have loved her horses like Matthew loves Trump and Spade."

The Morgan horses listened closely as Pounce spoke, and then they nodded their heads up and down slowly as though they knew how the old lady felt about her family horses.

Catcher also nodded as he spoke. It gave him a warm kind of feeling even though he knew next to nothing about the topic, yet it was kind of Catcher and the horses to listen. He remembered how his mama had instructed him to listen politely when others spoke, and now here he was speaking and others were being polite to him. *Mama kitty, I feel good,* popped into his little cathead.

Catcher waved one paw in the air as she continued talking and Pounce was caught up in more of the Morgan history. "Years later, they were the favorite mounts of American Cavalry officers. These big fellows come from a famous family of horses."

She rattled on some more about strong horses with great hearts charging across open battlefields, or dragging canons and pulling wagons or, most amazing of all, standing steady under gunfire. "Today, most people just ride them and even police forces use them. Did you know that they can jump fences and do cross country races, too? Matthew gets a magazine with lots of pictures of Morgan horses doing all sorts of things, and he's always telling Bonny about it. I've seen lots of the pictures when he's left the magazines out."

Pounce was growing used to the cadence in which she spoke when she was trying to teach him something. It was musical and awoke the poetic part of him, so he listened attentively and waited for more.

"Trump and Spade are old-time working Morgan horses. See how their necks arch so strongly, and how little their ears are, and how broad their faces?" Catcher seemed lost as she studied her friends while a big smile played on her little pussycat face. "Those black manes and tails, black legs, and that rich earthy brown color? Their coloring is called bay. These are bay horses. Aren't they handsome fellows?"

"Aw, Catcher," Trump swung his head over and looked at her.

"Huuu," Spade blew. "You're embarrassing us now."

The tails of both horses swished and brushed down their smooth coats, driving away small insects.

"Well, my good friends, it's true. You are beautiful fellows and I've a job to do. I'm to take Pounce all over the farm and make sure he knows all about us. He must get ready to live in the barn and catch mice."

"Of course. We understand. Spade and me, well, we'll do anything we can to help Pounce learn his way on the farm. You've told him, of course, about the old silo? Where he cannot go?"

"No, not yet. That's for another day."

"Well, son," Spade drawled out, "you listen up when she tells you about the silo. None of us go there. And that's that!"

"Yes, Pounce. None of us go there." This last was snorted by Trump as he arched his neck and blew hard in the cat's direction and then stomped the ground with one of his front feet for emphasis.

Pounce went from completely relaxed to tensed and arched again.

"There, there. Don't frighten our city kitty, fellows. I'll tell him everything he needs to know in time. Bye for now."

Catcher gave a warm glance back as the two cats trotted off across the pasture toward the barn. The horses sent a long "Who-eee" in reply.

"Aren't they lovely, Pounce? There are lots of horses bigger and taller, but because our friends have so many muscles, they look bigger than they are."

Pounce was shocked. "Horses bigger than those guys?" He shuddered but Catcher didn't notice. She continued to speak dreamily about her horse friends. Pounce listened but now with only half a mind for he had become troubled about something else besides the size of the horses.

"What's a silo?"

"Silos are buildings used to store silage. That's the chopped corn and other cut-up vegetation that men pack into them. It ferments in there for awhile and then it's fed to the cattle."

"Ugh. Sounds awful."

"Yes, I'm sure it is, except to a cow. You know the tall, round building next to the north end of our barn?"

"Yes."

"That's Matthew's old silo, but he doesn't make silage since he sold his dairy cows. The last of his silage was trucked away when the dairy cows left. I think Mr. Svensen took it last fall, but I can't remember. I was too busy healing up in the house then."

"How do you know these things?"

"The cows tell me, and they learned it from the big steers down in the north end of the pasture. You've not met those cattle yet. Matthew will keep them penned until they leave in a few months. They are kind of wild, so we won't get close to them."

"Okay, but what about the old silo? What were the horses talking about?"

They had arrived at the door of the barn. Catcher stopped and looked at Pounce with a long, warm gaze. "Some things are better left for a full telling and showing, my citified friend. At the right time, I'll tell you everything you need to know. Good night, you innocent little city cat." She chuckled as she disappeared into the dark interior of the barn.

Pounce turned toward the house. He was suddenly apprehensive of what the horses had inferred and he did not purr in Bonny's lap that night. Instead, after his dinner he got up into his dresser drawer bed and pondered the information he'd learned. *What agitated the horses when they talked about the silo? What was there to make even those big animals cautious? And why wouldn't Catcher tell him right away?*

He lay awake a long time before falling into a restless sleep where he dreamed about a tall, round building filled with dark, rotting vegetation. In the background he seemed to hear moos from the cows and snorts and stamping from the horses.

Bonny watched her sleeping and twitching cat before she went to bed herself. His attitude that evening had bothered her but pleased Matthew. She felt something was wrong and Matthew felt that the cat was finally becoming an outdoor cat.

Pounce continued to dream and twitch even after the house was full of human snoring. Finally, when his dream included seeing the amusing eyes of a little grey and silver cat, Pounce settled into a restful sleep.

CHAPTER 8

Silo Secret

Hay ripened in the fields. Matthew not only got several cuttings that summer but also occasionally took an early afternoon off to fish in the deepest parts of Rocky River. The trout seemed to love the area where Brawny had stood up to his chest in water eating grass from the overhanging bank. On that same bank Matthew set up his campstool, sat down in his barn overalls, and dangled his fishing line in the water while Wally lounged alongside.

Whenever Bonny saw Matthew take down his fishing pole and head toward the river, she'd wait an hour or two and then walk out to meet him with a jug of fresh squeezed lemonade and cold chicken sandwiches. The cats followed Bonny when she carried chicken down to the river. The smell of cooked chicken was too compelling to resist and Bonny often fed them tiny bites while she and Matthew ate lunch.

Pounce's life changed on one of those summer days. Early that morning Bonny had plucked him off a soft rug and placed him outside. Though still a little cool out, the sun had begun to warm both the air and ground. The cows were munching hay when he walked up to Matthew who rewarded him with a squirt of warm milk. Then he moved out of the way as Matthew gave milk to the Yellow Boys.

Blackie was still wild but Matthew put milk in a dish for her and her kittens, carried it around the corner, and set it down in the kitten hole. He paused a moment to pet the tumbling large kittens while Blackie stayed up in the rafters, but she came down after he left and disappeared into the kitten hole.

Pounce joined Catcher on the top of a stall rail while Matthew talked softly to the horses as he fed them and brushed their coats. When he turned them out of their stalls for the river pasture, Pounce and Catcher said goodbye to the big fellows, giving a soft body rub against their noses. *It's nice being on the stall rail*, Pounce thought. *No big hooves near my tail and their breath is so warm. Ahhh.*

Both cats followed Matthew as he fed the chickens and put grain and something really sloppy into the trough in the large pigpen. But Pounce and Catcher stayed away from those animals. Catcher had already warned Pounce that pigs could be danger-ous, and Bonny didn't want the cats pawing at the baby chicks or upsetting the hens.

"Pounce, that pig is Lady. Matthew says she weighs over sev-en hundred pounds." Catcher nodded toward the front of Lady's pigpen and that was the only introduction Pounce received but he didn't mind since he had no intention of getting close to that huge white bulk lounging inside the rails.

"How much is that?"

I don't know but it must be a lot. Has Bonny weighed you in the house?"

"Yes."

"Well, she weighed me too when I was healing. She told Matthew that it was important to monitor my weight to see if I was staying healthy."

"That's what she told him when I went on the scale."

"I bet he growled about it. Right?"

"Yup. He shouted. 'Don't put that cat up on the food scale!'"

Catcher giggled and finished the story they both knew. "But, dear, I wash it after weighing the cat."

Both cats laughed, but then Catcher added. "You know, Pounce, you were awfully thin when you arrived here and I'm glad Bonny was watching your health."

"Yup. She has taken good care of this hairless boy."

Catcher giggled as they passed the pigs and Lady only grunted but Pounce had heard grunts before, so he figured that was how pigs talked. There were a few noisy squeals from her large piglets as they trod on one another but that was all.

The cats followed Matthew to the bullpen where they watched from a distance as he fed and groomed the bull. Matthew led the bull around and around in the pen and petted him over and over.

Pounce was afraid of the bull because he tossed his head and made blowing sounds. But Brawny was good to look at, at least as good looking as the cows. He was tall and striking in his black and white coat. He also had that wide stripe of white hair growing down the middle of his back. His small horns, not as long as the cows' horns, curled up and in toward one another.

Like the little black and white calf in the barn, Brawny had a black nose, a black topknot of hair growing between his ears, and his front legs were black with some mottled patches of white. Matthew kept talking to him like a pet dog. "Good boy. I can hardly wait to show you off at the fair, you funny fellow, you. And your fancy calves next year too. Ah, ah."

About that time Wally returned from taking the cows to the bottom of their pasture where the grass was thick and green. The bovines would spend most of the day eating their way up toward the barn. By midday they would be dozing and chewing their cuds under a stand of trees and would be at least halfway home before evening milking.

Wally and Matthew headed up to the house for breakfast. Pounce felt a twinge of desire to go up where the bacon was cooking since he hadn't eaten yet, but Catcher motioned for him to follow so he turned and followed this silver wonder that had so captured his heart.

"I have to take you somewhere today, Pounce, and it will take awhile so we better get started now."

It was a beautiful day for a walk. The sun had risen and was doing its duty by warming the air and drying off the night dew that still clung to the grass and bushes. The cats ambled through the pasture and then turned to walk up along the flowing river. It was noisy as usual, but this time Pounce enjoyed watching the water splash over and around the rocks.

They walked a long time before Catcher stopped. "Let's rest here, Pounce, while I tell you what you will see."

Pounce dropped onto the soft grass under a group of willow trees whose long, flowing branches hung out over the water. The sunlight, diffused by the moving leaves, danced in the ripples of Rocky River and sparkled its bright reflection back onto the cats.

Both cats were quiet and studied the lovely scene.

Then Catcher spoke. "This is a very old farm, Pounce. And Matthew and Bonny have two houses on this farm. Upstream is the original homestead."

"Homestead?"

"Well, I heard Matthew and Bonny talking to a man who came from some place called a county extension service. He came to talk about crops."

Catcher noticed that Pounce had his brow furrowed in puzzlement for he was stuck on one word. She grinned up at him from where she lay and began to explain, beginning with the last thought first. "He came to talk about crop rotation. One year the farmers plant one kind of crop. Then they plant something else the following year, or maybe a year after that. He said doing it that way was really important so that the land will be healthy and not dry up. Sometimes they even plant crops just for the land. That is, they don't harvest them at all. They just plow them under the soil again."

"Wow. What a waste."

"Well, I guess it used to seem that way to lots of farmers too. But this man was an old man, and he told Matthew about a time when farms had dusty fields during really dry years, and Matthew remembers his father talking about the dust bowl days though he never experienced them."

"Ha. Dust bowls. That's funny. Why would anyone want a bowl of dust?"

"Pounce, are you teasing me?" Catcher studied her companion's large honest eyes and realized that he just did not understand. Sighing, she continued to enlighten her city friend. "It's this way, Pounce. There were years when some places in this country were so dry that the winds lifted the soil and carried away. It got really dusty and some homes and farms were buried in dirt. People had to leave their homes and move away."

"That bad, huh?"

"Yes, that bad. After that, men learned how to protect the land by planting rows of trees and rotating crops and letting the land lie idle from time to time."

Before Pounce could open his mouth to insert another question or comment, she explained.

"When land is idle it means farmers are not plowing it. They let grass grow over it and let it rest. The agent said it's common for farmers to do that now and the land everywhere is healthier. Then Matthew told the man how hard it is for a small farmer to let his land be idle or unproductive for a year. You know, a farmer like Matthew needs his hay crop just to feed his animals, and he does sell some of that, but I guess he doesn't plant the corn and things he did years ago for he told the man about acres that he leaves in grass all the time now."

"Why? Why does he do that?"

"I think because he's older and the work is hard and without his dairy cows, he doesn't need to plant as much now. At least, that's what Bonny tells him. Anyway, before the man left, he and Matthew talked about the history of this farm and it was exciting to listen in."

"You must be a good listener, Catcher, for you are teaching me a lot." Pounce really meant the compliment, but Catcher wondered slightly if she was boring him, yet she continued.

"Homesteading is how most of this land was settled a long time ago when it was still wild. Men and women camped out on the land they wanted and put in some crops and built a barn and a house. Every year they did more work and planted more crops. After a few years, they were allowed to fill out some papers. If they did everything on the land that the government asked them to do during those years, they became the owners of it. This place was once a homestead like that."

"Oh, I see." He didn't really understand of course, but Catcher had a great mind for facts. So he figured she knew what she was talking about.

"Well, here's the scoop, Pounce. The old homestead is up this river and it was built long ago, I think by Matthew's great grandfather. Now, some of the buildings have fallen in from great age and there is an old silo."

"The silo. That's where we're going? But I thought ..."

Catcher interrupted him. "Pounce, you are right. This is a forbidden and dangerous place and we will not get close. But we may get to see something that should not be there. An enemy of Matthew's lives there. That is why the animals won't go up there to graze."

"Wow! An enemy? Like those bad boys who burned me? Or the coyote that chased me?"

"Oh, Pounce, I'm so sorry. You didn't tell me boys burned you. How naughty of them."

"They weren't naughty, Catcher, they were mean spirited. And they were not little children, but older boys on bicycles. Almost men!" Pounce's voice was suddenly hard and his eyes narrowed as he sat up. "It was a burning garbage pit they threw me in and a bicycle wheel that hurt my ribs."

Catcher uttered a little compassionate groan, "Mm," and reached forward to lick Pounce on the side of his face as though to lick away the memory.

"It's okay, Catcher. I'm getting over it now." Pounce dropped down again beside her.

Catcher sighed and then continued. "Listen, Pounce, this enemy is much worse and more dangerous than any enemy you have ever faced. This enemy is worse than my old owner, too. This enemy is a cat."

"Ha, ha. You're funny, Catcher. A cat! As if a cat can be worse than a coyote. Ha, ha."

His momentary anger instantly forgotten, he hooted with delight and rolled over, his white belly hair sparkling even whiter in the sunlight.

Catcher waited until Pounce grew quiet again. Then she looked him straight in the eyes. "Pounce. You must listen to me. This is no joke."

He sat up and put his head forward. "You really mean it, don't you?"

"Yes, Pounce. I really mean it. For our safety, you must listen to me and not be silly about what you do not understand."

Instantly sobered, Pounce waited quietly. His friend was beginning to frighten him now. Her eyes had darkened and she was no longer sprawled on the grass, but crouched with her very posture indicating readiness in danger.

"It's like this. In the wilderness there are wild cats. Not like Blackie whose family was once tame and lived like we do, *you know*," she winced, "with people. These cats have never been tamed and they are very large."

"Bigger than the coyotes?"

"Yes."

"Bigger than Wally?"

"Yes, Pounce. Bigger than Wally."

Pounce was silent for Wally was a very large collie, as collies go. "Does Matthew know that he has a big cat enemy living on his farm?"

"No Pounce. He doesn't know where it is. He only knows there is one in the county. These cats are big enough to kill calves, and sometimes horses and cows too."

These cats are big enough to kill calves, and sometimes horses and cows too." She lowered her voice and whispered. "I heard Matthew tell the extension service man that a very long time ago a cougar, that's what they are called, hurt a man in the county. I think it was in his grandfather's day, but I don't know."

Pounce drew his breath in sharply. He tried to digest all of this awful information. He was a chicken gravy, cushion-loving house-cat, and he didn't want to hear this. But Catcher was in charge of his education now. So he waited, and remained quiet, even though it made his chest hurt to hold his breath and think unpleasant things. Catcher could tell that he was somewhat distressed. She put her nose against his for a moment and then continued with the rest of her lesson.

"These large wild cats are hard to spot because their coat color is like the grass in fall and the ground they walk on. They blend in really well. They usually live far away in the wilderness but they like living on the edge of farmland because of what they consider," Catcher exhaled, "easy prey."

"What now, Catcher?" Pounce shook his head as he spoke. He wanted to dislodge her words, but they were already implanted and he could not escape their painful meaning.

"Now, you must listen carefully. We will be drawing near very soon and I want you to walk really softly. Then I'll show you something. Let's rest and sleep a bit since we'll need to be alert."

Catcher curled up and in a just a few blinks was fast asleep.

It took Pounce a little while longer, but the warmth from the dappled sunlight and the noise from Rocky River lulled him into his midday snooze as well.

Several hours later, when the two refreshed cats awoke, they had a drink of water and walked on. In and out of the brush by the river they walked. The water splashing over the stones covered any slight rustle they made in passing and the felines were careful to weave in and out of the shadows cast by the overhanging brush and trees.

When Catcher began to walk at a crouch, Pounce followed her lead and did the same thing. Pounce found that he was holding his breath as he thought about the big wild cat.

Stop it, he thought. *Now breathe deep, kitty-cat, and be brave, just like your mama taught you. In, out. In, out. Ah, there.* He exhaled loudly as he stood up straight.

"That's better," he said in a normal tone.

"Hiss … Pounce. Quiet. These big cats can hear anything." Catcher hissed at him again. She sounded vexed, and Pounce dropped again to his crouch and this time he remembered to breathe.

After walking some distance, they skirted the edge of another pasture that grew down to the large boulders lining that part of the river. This was open ground, so the cats hurried across it and stayed close to the water as they scampered around the rocks to reach a large woodlot running east and west. The thick tangle of pine trees and the smaller trees in the open areas butted up along the crashing river where several fallen trees jutted out over the water. The woodlot continued on the other side of the river to the west.

Catcher stopped under a fallen pine log whose branches lay in the river, causing the water to swirl in every direction. Pounce had learned frightening news on this journey, yet he still had no idea of how dangerous it was, and his mind wandered. He wanted to study the swirling water around the branches in the river, but Catcher's eyes were dark and her expression demanded his attention.

She whispered, though the sound of water on rocks stole some of her words away. "Stop. We'll climb this ... tree. It's big enough to hold us but ... small for the big cat. When I go up, follow me up to ... branch. See? That ... above us?"

Catcher was whispering so low that Pounce could hardly hear her. She had her mouth right up against his head, and he felt almost giddy when he scented her breath and looked closely into her deep green eyes. He turned his head and his whiskers rubbed under her chin. Then he breathed her scent in deeply and exhaled loudly which caused her to once again warn him. "Shhh." But this time there was a puzzled look in her eyes when she looked at him. She shook her head and began to slowly climb the pine tree.

Both cats were grateful for the noisy river below them when their claws made some scratching noises as they went up. Tiny pieces of pine bark fell, but they hardly noticed so intent were they to reach the designated branch. Pounce felt the rough bark against his hide as he brushed against the branches they passed. He felt where Bonny had stitched his hip but that was only because he had scar tissue under the hair that had grown over it. The excitement he felt was too intense for him to give it much notice. Soon they gained the large branch where Catcher instructed Pounce to sit as close to the trunk as he could. She climbed a foot higher and sat down on another branch that was angled a little away from Pounce.

She whispered again. "Pounce, you must stay still until I tell you otherwise. Don't make any noise, no matter what you see. When it is safe, I will lead us back down and home. Do you understand me?"

His affirmative nod was all the answer she needed. One last whisper from Catcher and then all grew quiet in the pine tree. Both cats remained motionless and waited.

While they waited Pounce began to study the scene before him through the thick branches and needles of the pine. There was the old homestead. A small cabin, mostly fallen in, and a corral attached to a leaning barn stood half in and half out of the high grass. The fields around the place looked beautiful to Pounce. *Full of mice I bet,* he mused. *Look at that thick, tall grass. They like to hide in there.* The fields were indeed lovely and completely surrounded the place. The late afternoon sun made the seed heads on the grass glimmer as they waved in the warm breeze. *Wow,* Pounce thought. *The cows and Spade and Trump would love this.*

From his vantage point up in the tree he could see, next to the right side of the barn, the object of their attention and their journey—the silo, the infamous silo the animals were warned about. Pounce turned his attention to it and studied it. He had expected something much larger, but this silo was a small, round building made from split pine boards standing on end that were bound with iron rings. A ladder built on the outside of the silo went all the way up to the top. The entire building was not as tall as the Larsen barn.

There was a door opening at the bottom of the silo, but the heavy door was half off, still partly attached by one hinge. The tree cats had a clear view of the south-facing opening. Several small openings covered in wire were evenly spaced around the silo near the top. The roof itself was a funny inverted bowl shape. Its metal was shining in the sun and Pounce could see something that looked like horseshoes mounted all over the top. *What are they doing up there?* He wondered but then also wondered how anyone could be afraid of it. In fact, the dark opening of the door was inviting to a cat and to Pounce it looked like it needed exploring.

While he thought about how he would love to look around inside, part of the field grass to the northwest of the buildings began to ripple. The breeze was not making that singular path of movement! Pounce leaned forward to study the motion and he didn't have long to wait.

The strange waving of the grass continued as though being

parted. It bent in swells and swirls toward the open area near-est the cabin. Both cats stiffened in the tree and tried to push their bodies even closer to the trunk. Staring straight ahead all they could see was the tall waving grass. Suddenly the tall grass parted, and a huge, tawny colored cougar stepped out. She was carrying something brown and white in her mouth. Pounce was shocked when he recognized that something as a small goat be-longing to the Bensons who lived just north of the Larsen farm. It was dead.

On Saturday afternoons the Bensons often stopped on their way home from the market in town to visit Matthew and Bonny. The cats knew the Bensons and some of their brown and white goats and even a few of their miniature cattle because, while the people talked farming and drank coffee on the porch, Wally and the cats visited whatever animals were in their truck. These good folks liked cats, and Catcher and Pounce had also spent many an hour curled up in their ample laps during these late afternoon coffee visits. There they heard of goat-milking demonstrations at the market, and all about how to make goat cheese. Sometimes they learned about a miniature calf that had sold. The goats they met at the truck were always polite, but rather simple. Pounce had already decided that goats, like cows, had no poetry in their souls so it was hard to get to know one well.

What he saw now was terrible. This was tragic and Pounce felt strange all over. *Was this a goat he had met at the Bensons' truck?* Fear and rage tightened every muscle in his small cat body. Gripping the tree branch with all of his claws, he flattened his ears on his head and his body on his branch. Catcher was flat-tened in the same way just a foot away on her branch. The cats barely breathed.

The cougar paused and sniffed, then continued until she was completely out of the tall grass. She walked in front of the cabin toward the barn. Behind her the grass continued to rustle and move. Then two half-grown cougar kittens burst out into the open. They were much larger than the cats up the tree, but still kittens. Their mouths were moving and they were vocalizing, but the cats could not hear the sound of their cougar mews over the noise of Rocky River at their feet. The large cougar walked straight ahead, her long, heavy tail just inches above the ground. Past the barn she walked carrying her kill, her head lifted high to keep it above the ground. Then she disappeared into the dark opening of the silo. Her kittens followed and all was again quiet.

The sun was down and the long shadows were now fading. After a few more moments, Catcher whispered, "Follow me, Pounce."

Both cats eased themselves as quietly as possible backwards down the tree. Then they hurried in the developing darkness toward home. They traveled quickly for a good distance before Catcher stopped and turned to Pounce. It was now very dark out and the pupils of her eyes were fully dilated.

"That is why you must never go near the silo! That is a mountain lion, a cougar. She is not where anyone expects her to be. Her place is in the mountains far from here, where everything is still wild. This dangerous cougar has moved into the farmlands and has found the silo. Now she hunts farm animals."

Catcher was trembling as she spoke, so Pounce drew near and licked her face to comfort her. He was shaking inside just as much as Catcher trembled on the outside.

"Pounce, listen to me. Like I said, a cougar sometimes will kill large animals like horses and cows. They are mostly afraid of dogs but little cats like us are easy prey for them. Now, she will stay in the silo for hours since she's feeding and nursing her kittens."

Catcher sighed as she thought soberly about what the big cougar and her kittens were eating that night. "After that they will sleep, and then, early in the morning, she will come out and take her kittens to drink down at the stream. Then they will sleep most of the day and perhaps hunt again tomorrow evening."

The cats started home silently. They were wrapped in their own thoughts and occasionally looked back over their shoulders. As they neared their own barn, they could hear Bonny on the steps of the house calling. "Pounce, Pounce, where are you?"

Catcher nosed Pounce a good night and turned into the barn. She seemed very, very sad. Pounce waited until she was out of sight, then turned toward Bonny and the warm, open door of the house.

Pounce did not purr on Bonny's lap that night. Instead, he ate his supper and hopped up into his dresser drawer where he curled up into a tight ball. Bonny was puzzled at his behavior but pleased that he was safe at home once again. She petted him in his drawer bed and studied his black and white head, but Pounce didn't raise it or purr. Now it was Bonny's turn to wonder if Pounce was becoming a barn cat after all and preferring to live outside.

She hesitated and looked down again at her little charge. Then patting him once more, she turned and went into her own bedroom where Matthew was already snoring.

Pounce lay awake long into the night. He was very, very angry.

CHAPTER 9

Preposterous Plan

Tired in the morning from his short night, Pounce lay quietly in his dresser bed, thinking. His rage and anger had settled into a firm feline determination to do something about what he had seen the day before. Resolved to act, he quietly got down and asked to go outside early, even before breakfast.

"Mer-rouw," he said, looking up at Bonny.

"Pounce? The farm is barely awake yet, and don't you want breakfast with me?" She wondered if he was feeling all right for it wasn't like Pounce to skip breakfast, and two mornings in a row at that. Leaning over and giving him a quick pat, she stood up again and studied her healthy looking, and well recovered, pussycat.

Pounce mewed quietly again at the door, and Bonny dutifully opened it. He didn't hurry but neither did he amble. His steps were direct and purposeful as he padded toward the barn where he watched as Matthew and Wally finished up the chores. Pounce then whispered to the big collie as the man and dog passed him on their way to the house.

"Wally, sir. May I have a word with you this morning?"

Wally stopped and looked at the cat quizzically. That was the most respectful request a cat had ever directed toward him. He was quite taken back by it, but then smiled in his friendly collie fashion and put his nose out as though to use typical feline manners in greeting the cat. Pounce extended his nose too but stopped short of touching the dog.

"Haw, cat. Gonna get along I see." Matthew grunted with satisfaction when he saw the dog and cat nosing toward each other in a friendly fashion.

"Of course, little cat." Wally replied, still smiling but now wondering if a cat could say anything important. "Would you mind if I have a bite of breakfast first? I've had an early start and these old bones are in need of nourishment."

"Yes, sir. Would you meet me here right after you eat? I have something to say to you."

Wally was intrigued and lifted his ears with interest. He nodded to Pounce and continued behind Matthew to the house.

Catcher was sitting behind the barn door listening to this strange conversation and she stuck her head out after Wally moved on. "Good morning, Pounce, and what was that about?"

Pounce moved over to where she sat and lightly touched her nose, breathed in her scent, and smiled at her. Something had happened to him and Catcher could sense it. *He seems confident and taller*, she thought. *Hmm, that's funny. Why would I think that?* Pounce seemed to have grown up overnight and she sensed something different about him.

He sat down next to her. "Catcher, I am going to speak to Wally about something important this morning. And you," he smiled warmly at her, "will you sit by my side when I do?"

This time it was Catcher who felt giddy when he spoke. He seemed to need her. Yet something about his manner let her know that he also wanted to protect her. Sitting by his side was more than his need; it was to meet her need and she knew it. If cats can blush, Catcher did. She felt an immediate love rise in her for this funny, still mostly ignorant, house cat.

"Yes, Pounce, I will stay by you." She lowered her beautiful green eyes as she nodded.

He didn't miss the change in words. He had asked her to sit by him and she had answered that she would stay by him. It made his heart beat faster, but he pushed his deepening affection for her down and refocused on the task at hand. "Will you get Blackie and the Yellow Boys and tell them that there is a meeting in the front of the barn?"

Catcher trotted off at once and Pounce sat down to wait for Wally. He was not long in returning. When the big collie arrived, he sat down in front of Pounce just as the other cats arrived.

"Well, cat. What is this all about?"

Pounce suddenly felt very small in the presence of the strong dog and the hunting barn cats. Nevertheless, he drew himself up to his full twelve pounds of soft house cat and began. "Sir, it's like this. I have seen the silo and its inhabitant, the cougar."

The Yellow Boys crouched and hissed at the word, and Blackie sat very still with her ears pinned back against her head. Only Catcher seemed perfectly calm as she sat by Pounce's side.

Wally narrowed his eyes and growled slowly. "You knew, didn't you, cat? You were not to go near the silo."

"I took him, Wally," Catcher said slowly.

Wally swung his big ruffled neck toward Catcher and barked. "Catcher! What were you thinking? Don't you know what a loss to Bonny you would be?" Then, in a softer voice, as Catcher cowered in front of him, he continued. "It would have been a great loss for all of us."

"Oh, Catcher." Blackie whispered as she walked up and licked her friend's face. "What were ya thinking, girl?"

Catcher remained where she was on the ground. Then Pounce moved closer to her and put one paw on her shoulder. "Friends, don't blame her. She was under orders to show me the entire farm. Catcher thought that she needed to reinforce the warning I had received about the silo with a little fear. I, you know, being a silly house cat and not country wise as you are. At first I didn't even believe her. She told me that a cat is able to kill a cow. I laughed." Pounce paused, lowered his head and in a softer voice continued. "I thought it was a joke."

Wally watched him, his forehead furrowed and his lips tight with anger. The others restrained themselves from further comment while they waited to see what Wally would say and why they had been asked to gather. Pounce continued where he had left off and, once again, Catcher was amazed at him. He seemed to be expressing himself with remarkable clarity of thought.

"After seeing the cougar who, by the way, has two half-grown kittens, we returned. I did not sleep much last night. I could not get out of my mind the image of that beast carrying her kill into the silo. I saw it clearly. It was a brown and white goat from the Benson farm up north. Maybe," he looked down and sighed, "even one that we had met here on the farm."

The Yellow Boys started growling among themselves and moving restlessly on the scattered floor straw. Wally shot them a hard look, and they instantly ceased and grew quiet again.

"Go on, cat," Wally said slowly, his eyes narrow and hard.

"I believe I've devised a plan to rid ourselves of the danger and return the homestead fields to our family." This last was said quietly. Even Pounce understood, that with this comment he had embraced the Larsen couple and all the animals on the farm as his family. He knew it meant he might have to live in the barn and spend the rest of his life watching out for horse hooves and rampaging bulls. But he had decided to do what he felt was right. And that was that.

The Yellow Boys rolled over on the straw in the aisle and began to snicker, but Blackie calmly stepped over to them and put her face down very close to theirs. She spoke in a slow, menacing whisper and deliberately let her whiskers brush across their faces. "You give the city cat respect and let him talk. Or I'll tear out yer soft yellow bellies, and feed 'um to my kits one bite at a time. You git my meaning? This boy, this boy cat done saw da cougar. Git it?"

The Yellow Boys lay still and nodded that they got it. They thought she would not really tear out their bellies, but they couldn't be absolutely sure. Both cats nodded even more vigorously as Blackie stared them into submission. When she was satisfied they would comply, she sat down, blew her breath out sharply, and gave a quick lick to one front leg. She looked back at Pounce expectantly.

"Get to the point, cat. I've work to do and cows to watch." Wally spoke with impatience, angry at the cats for their folly.

"Sir, I think, if all the animals will work together, we can do something about this problem. If you will allow me, I have something to suggest."

At this point Pounce did something none of the animals expected. He walked up close to the big collie's face and spoke quietly. "May I speak to you privately for a moment?"

Wally nodded, stood up and walked a few feet away, then dropped down on his belly.

"Come here, kid. Tell me in this old ear. No. This one. It's still got the best hearing."

Pounce stepped over Wally's front paws and then began to whisper in Wally's left ear while the cats waited. Wally frowned at first. Then he looked amazed. Then he pulled his head back and looked intently at the cat. "Well!"

Then he lowered his head again and listened some more. Finally he nodded and stood up and both animals returned to the others. "Cats, it's like this. Pounce has a preposterous plan that just might work. He's asked me to undertake its execution and to spearhead the details. As farm guard dog, I accept the challenge. The large animals will listen to me. We all know how much this farm means to our owners, the Larsens. Let's do it for them."

Wally was a formidable dog. Even though Catcher and the Yellow Boys and Blackie had no idea what *it* was that they would do for Matthew and Bonny, out of respect for Wally they nodded yes in spite of the sizable fear growing in them.

The words had rolled off Wally's tongue in his clipped fashion and his eyes glinted with determination and another look that was frightening to the cats. They could not understand what it meant to have the responsibility of protecting everything on the farm.

However, the city cat had somehow tapped into a concept normally beyond a feline mind. Pounce had grasped the idea that each animal, not only those belonging to the Larsens, but also those belonging to their neighbors, had value.

It was very un-catlike, since felines normally only think of themselves, their kittens, and their territorial range. To want to help other species was rare in a cat. It was what motivated canines to protect cattle and sheep and serve their masters. It was this trait that caught Wally's attention as Pounce spoke to him

Wally continued, "When I was young, the big cats came onto our land. I saw a milk cow on another farm that a big cat had bitten and torn. It was a sad day around here. To bring them to justice, Matthew took me on a hunt along with other men and their dogs. We drove two big cats up into trees where the murderous things were shot with darts, caged, and carried away. One young female escaped to the high country. It might be that one who's here in our silo."

The cats sat trembling and still. Shock that Wally had actually hunted cougars rolled over them. This dog truly was their friend and protector. His story caused their estimation of him to soar. As relatively small animals, they would never dream of hunting something bigger than themselves. Wally stood and shook himself, making his white ruff appear even bigger.

"Matthew says farmers and ranchers are not allowed to kill a predator like a cougar unless they actually see one killing their livestock." This last sentence was growled for he had often listened to Matthew talk to his friends about how difficult it would be to actually see a predator kill livestock that are scattered through many fields and over many acres filled with stands of trees, hills, and rock outcroppings. His growl caused all the cats to crouch in front of him with their ears back, so Wally composed himself and attempted a softer look, but only managed to cover some of his teeth as he continued to speak.

"In the meantime, as Pounce saw, farmers in this area are steadily losing livestock, one precious animal at a time. It's hard to prove that a big cat took them because of the weather, the way they often move their victim to another location, and other reasons. Most of the time we don't even find the bones of the dead."

The cats looked at Wally with wide eyes; that is, all except Blackie. She seemed calm, though very angry. Pounce wondered if she also had seen the big cat. She caught his eye and barely nodded. Pounce's respect for this wild black cat went up.

Wally paused and bowed his head a moment and the cats did the same, knowing that they must show respect for the animals that had lost their lives in such a horrible way. Then Wally went on talking about farming, and ranching, and guard dogs. He even mentioned that some farms have donkeys to help guard sheep and goats. Pounce was not sure what a donkey was. Turning to Catcher to ask her about donkeys, he started to open his mouth but she answered before he could speak.

"Shh ..." Thus Catcher let him know without looking at him that Wally had more to say, and it would be wise for Pounce to hold his bunny-trail thoughts until later. Pounce closed his mouth and was still again.

Wally did not like making speeches, but this was different. He, the guardian animal, knew that if nothing was done, it was just a matter of time before one of them would be missing. Finally, he took a deep breath and said one last thing. "Now, we have stopped using all of our fields because we cannot safely patrol them with just old Matthew and old me doing the work. It has not been easy."

Wally paused and looked around at the cats. He had not intended to tell them this much, especially about cougar hunts in the past. He had not shared this information with the horses or cows either, except to warn them not to graze the north pastures. However, there is a time for everything, and now was the time for the animals to know the facts surrounding this wild predator.

Pounce had motivated him, and he was beginning to feel like a young dog again.

Something exciting was coming and his eyes glinted with anticipation. What Pounce had whispered to him made sense, and the accompanying look that was forming on the dog's face began to frighten the cats. Wally saw their reaction and attempted to soften his features again, as well as his voice.

"This house cat has displayed remarkable presence of mind with his idea. Now, together we will execute it. The animals of the Larsen farm will do what we should have done long ago." Wally growled out his command. "Cats. You stay here until I return. The horses and cows must be informed of their part in this plan.

"Blackie, you stay with your kittens until I call you. Yellow Boys, no hunting today. Go up into the rafters and wait for me. Don't let Matthew or Bonny see you. Pounce, you and Catcher loll around on the bales as you usually do. Let's give Matthew nothing to wonder about as we make our plans. I'll be back to tell you what you will be expected to do."

Wally turned sharply and trotted off around the barn to cross the pasture, and then to head south toward the bend in the river where the cows and horses were grazing. In route he stopped and briefly spoke to the bull in his pen. It must have been effective because Brawny bellowed loudly and began pawing and huffing as Wally left for the river.

The cats didn't move from where they were. They crouched, silent and somewhat apprehensive, listening to Brawny tearing up the ground and huffing in his pen alongside the barn. Pounce forgot about donkeys.

CHAPTER 10

Silo Caper

The day finally arrived. It was a Saturday when Wally told the animals the plan would be carried out, but he didn't tell them until after the milking and chores. By then he had learned that Matthew and Bonny planned to stay in town throughout the afternoon, and Wally thought that just might give the animals enough time to carry out their plan.

Matthew was sure that the cows and horses were just feeling frisky when they snorted and mooed as he turned them out into the pasture, but it was Wally's whispered words as they walked by the dog that caused that extra little kick in their step. By the time the farm truck carrying Matthew and Bonny left for town, the large animals were down by the river and too excited to graze, especially the cows. Wally had also told the cats in the barn and they were especially tense at the prospect of outsmarting their wild and dangerous cousin, the cougar. This was to be an adventure in courage for all the animals on the Larsen farm.

Wally barked at the animals by the river and they obeyed by gathering at the north end of the pasture near the fenced section for the steers. This was not far from where the east road ran alongside the pasture and where Matthew had driven the truck on the raccoon day. There the horses and cows waited for Wally to bring the bull, the pig, and the cats.

The older steers pressed for information but the cows ignored them since Wally had told them not to tell. This in itself was amazing since cows are not known for being able to keep secrets. However, on this ominous Saturday, apprehension about the events about to take place sealed the lips of the Randall cows and not one moo or bawl escaped them.

Wally's decision to leave the steers behind was a hard one because he felt they needed as large an animal army as possible. However, the young steers were prone to wild displays of exuberance, and the dog feared they might act up in some juvenile way and ruin the plan, endangering themselves or others. It was a risk Wally was not willing to take. Wally had rightly guessed that it would not be wise to tell the chickens because you could never tell what a chicken would do. Their brains were just too small to grasp the concept of a troop of farm animals taking on a cougar.

So, other than Pounce the housecat and the mostly grown Brawny, all the animals were reasonably seasoned and, hopefully, able to follow instructions and act responsibly.

The horses milled about, impatient to get moving. Occasionally Spade snorted and pawed the ground, but that just made the other animals even tenser.

"Brother. That will not get us moving any faster. You'll only work up a sweat. Now, cool it, bro. Come walk with me slowly. It will help our muscles relax." Trump spoke comfortably to his younger brother and Spade fell into step alongside him. They began cutting a few large and slow circles around the cows and it refocused all five of the animals.

At the barn meanwhile, Wally bemoaned his aging teeth as he gnawed through the bull's halter rope. "Brawny! Don't pull back on the rope. It hurts my mouth."

"Huugh," the bull replied. He eased up on the halter rope by moving closer to the post and, a moment later, the last strand separated.

Brawny broke out of his enclosure easily. Then it was his turn to free Lady out of her pen. He simply pushed on the gate with his head, the latch broke, the gate swung open, and Lady stepped out freely. Her piglets paid no attention to her walking away. They were large now and penned in their own pen next to hers. As Wally led Lady, Brawny and all five cats trailed behind until they joined the large animals assembled in the north corner of the big pasture.

Sunlight splashed off the coats of the cows, horses, cats, pig, bull, and dog as the mixed company walked single file. It was serious business yet, to any onlooker, it would have been a comical sight as the troop wound in and out among the trees and boulders that filled in gaps between pasture land and noisy Rocky River. Pounce was so caught up in the excitement of the whole idea that he immediately launched into a song.

"I've a plan, a pouncing plan, for the land, for the land.
I've a plan, a pouncing plan, for the land."

"Pounce! Be quiet now!" Wally growled at him as the other animals shook their heads and gave him narrow looks. So Pounce whispered the next line.

"I'm pouncing on the journey with my plan, I am.
I'm pouncing on the journey with my plan, I am."

"Shhh ..." Blackie shot back at him from where she walked behind Catcher. He grew quiet then and hummed the next line and the humming tickled his mouth. So he went back to whispering.

"When I get there with my friends, it will be the cougars' end.
I've a plan, a pouncing plan for the land.
FOR THE LAND!"

This last line was sung loudly and all the animals stopped and shouted, "POUNCE! BE QUIET!"

Trump eyed the little cat now cowering in front of them all, and then spoke softly to him. "It's a good thing we're too far away yet to be heard, son. Now be silent, and I'll let you ride the rest of the way. Cats. Come here. Get up on Spade and me and we'll make better time."

Trump's idea was gratefully accepted by the cats and, leaping up onto the horses' backs, they settled down for the ride. The swaying motion felt good to the cats and they loved being so high off the ground as they sat and looked around with bright eyes and swishing tails. It was exhilarating and they only had to duck once in a while to keep the low hanging branches from brushing them off.

Big Yellow and Blackie rode on Spade's rump and Little Yellow crouched and clung to Spade's withers.

"Easy cat," Spade whispered, twitching his skin. "Horse withers are tender. Put your front paws in my mane instead. Balance yourself. You're a cat."

Catcher and Pounce rode on Trump and sat very close together on his rump. After a while Catcher sighed and laid her head on Pounce's shoulder as they rode.

"Pounce?"

"Yes."

"I'm a little frightened by all of this. Are you sure ..." Her voice trailed off and she buried her nose in his neck as Trump swiveled one ear back to hear what they were saying.

"Catcher, I don't know anything for sure. But I know one thing. This evil beast must not be allowed to stay on the farm or it will mean death for some of the animals. Matthew is getting old now and Wally is already an old dog. Next spring the cows will have calves. And you know the sow will have another litter of pigs and look at all the little chickens we have running around and, and ..."

Catcher stopped him. "Yes, of course. I know," she sighed again deeply. "It's just that I don't want anything bad to happen to you."

Pounce's heart leaped in him as he looked into her beautiful face. Then he licked it from the tip of her nose right up to between her lovely ears.

"Catcher, I'll be fine. We all will. You'll see."

The entire troop covered the distance much faster now that they could take normal sized steps since the cats were riding. The cows were used to being herded and so they walked in front quietly, followed by the young bull and Wally. Melody walked softly and her bell did not ring. Then came the horses carrying the cats, and bringing up the rear was the sow.

Wally muttered to himself as they traveled. *This better work or I'm one dead collie dog, out here risking the lives of our livestock, the livestock I swore to guard with my life.* He swung his head back and forth, alert and watching for any sign of danger. The hair on his forehead was wrinkled in deep furrows and his lips moved as he muttered, but none of the animals could hear him.

They continued walking along Rocky River until they were within sight of the old homestead. The grass, trees, and boulders had concealed the troop well, and the roar from the water on the rocks covered the occasional clink of a horse's hoof. The cattle continued to walk silently and that surprised Pounce because they mooed so much at home. He thought that Wally would be telling them to be quiet for the entire trip.

Suddenly Wally called out softly. "Here, girls. Stop here."

The three cows didn't have to be told twice. It had been a while since Wally had driven them up from their favorite spot by the river, and the grass here was deep and green and inviting. They immediately dropped their heads and began to graze. The young bull moved in closer to them and began grazing alongside.

Wally flattened himself in the tall grass by the noisy water and then he whispered to the cattle. "Graze until I give you the word." Turning to the sow, the dog whispered, "Okay, Lady. You know what to do."

The massive white pig grunted quietly and then, without comment and without showing any signs of apprehension, moved out from behind the horses and began to deliberately walk toward the homestead by herself. The other animals stared after her with more interest than they had ever shown in her before. Pounce immediately wanted to write a brave pig song and could feel the tickle in his mouth to start humming but he restrained himself—barely. House cats don't usually exhibit the self-control their hunting cousins do, yet somehow in this tense and important situation, the city cat managed to do it.

Wally whispered again, now commanding. "Now, cats. Get off here. Sneak forward and climb into the trees where Pounce and Catcher were when they saw the cougar. Not a word from any of you." He glared at Pounce pointedly. "When I call, then you all know what is expected of you."

"Yes, sir," Pounce whispered as he hopped down from Trump's back. The rest of the cats dutifully followed him as he headed toward the stand of pine trees nearby. They all disappeared out of sight under the overhanging brush along the water.

Wally turned his attention to the horses. "Okay, boys. You two and I will move forward until we see Lady and then you fellows just quietly graze as though nothing else in the world mattered."

"Boo—off," Trump blew and his flanks quivered with uncertainty. Then he whispered. "Yes, Wally. But you know what big cat smell does to horses. This will be an exercise of horse willpower for sure." Turning to his brother he called softly, "Spade, we have work to do. Come on."

The horses moved off, followed slowly by Wally. He hung back, not wanting his dog smell to precede him. He breathed slowly and watched where he put his paws though the noise from the river was very loud as the water crashed against the boulders. Wondering if his white and gold coat could be seen from across the clearing, Wally crouched deeply into the high grass as he padded forward, stopping and holding his body still every few steps before moving on again. He could barely hear the hooves of the horses ahead of him. *This is good,* he thought. *And the breeze is coming from the northwest. The big cat won't be able to smell us. That is, if she's still hunting north of here.*

When they reached the clearing that lay in front of the old buildings, they could see Lady. She was nosing her way in the clearing as though looking for tender shoots. The grazing and nosing went on several hours, and then the cows rested close to the river while the horses stood and dozed by them, or tried to doze. Lady had by this time also plopped down in the yard and was sleeping on her side, though she slept lightly. Time moved slowly for the animals. Inner tension kept them alert though outwardly they appeared to be resting. This was the most self-control any of them had ever exhibited, and Wally was extremely proud of his friends.

Finally the sun dropped low enough in the western sky to make long, tree-shaped shadows snake across the clearing. Wally knew that the cougar and her kittens had been off sleeping somewhere near where they would hunt and would come back as soon as the big cat made an early evening kill. He wanted the farm animals positioned long before the big cats returned.

The horses quietly moved out into the clearing and away from the boulders along the river when Wally nodded to them. Not knowing what was going to happen, Wally didn't want any of his friends trapped between boulders. Now they stood just beyond the trees but not anywhere near the buildings. In the meantime, the cows and Brawny had grazed their way up from the river until they were near the clearing as well, but they stood just in front of the pine trees where the Larsen cats were hiding.

Wally watched with satisfaction as the animals placed themselves, then he turned and walked in a crouch to the pines at the edge of the clearing. He looked up into them but could not see the cats. "Cats," he whispered. "Where are you?"

"Here, sir." Pounce raised his head from a branch and looked directly down into Wally's eyes.

The dog stared up into the trees, squinted, and then he smiled. All the cats were silent as planned, and he could see no part of them except the head of Pounce. He nodded at Pounce who promptly withdrew and left the tree looking, once more, totally cat-less.

Wally lay down and waited. The horses grazed at the edge of the clearing and the cows mouthed the grass in front of him. The cows and Brawny stayed very close to where Wally lay, not wanting to be separated from their protector. He had a good view most of the time, though he had to study the far pasture grass on the other side of the clearing by looking under the bellies and around the legs of four nervous bovines.

After what seemed like a very long wait, the grass way out in the north pasture started waving. Pounce coughed quietly to Wally who lay below his tree, and Wally responded by creeping a few yards forward on his belly. It gave him a better view. From there he would see the cougars when they exited the field.

His nod to the cattle reminded them to keep their heads down, and his whisper steadied them. "Don't run when the cats come out of the high grass. Close your eyes and you won't be frightened."

The cows closed their eyes while their hearts beat hard though you could not tell by looking. They looked sleepy and content as they continued to graze with just their skin twitching from time to time. To an onlooker it would have appeared they were twitching bugs away and not trying, oh so hard, to remain calm.

Wally felt rather than heard the rumble beginning inside of Brawny whose eyes began to roll and who had started to lower his head in that characteristic *bull knows an enemy is near–bull plans on charging* stance. Wally remained silent, but showed his curled lips and white fangs to the bull and instantly Brawny changed his mind, closed his eyes, and stood as quiet and steady as the cows.

The sow reacted first by grunting loudly and got up as the big cat stepped from the field into the clearing alongside the old house. Lady kept grunting and backing slowly away from the middle of the clearing. The cougar froze and stared at the sow. She carried a large white goose in her mouth. The cats in their pine trees saw it all clearly, but it was nobody the cats had ever met so they sighed in relief. Then they felt a collective guilt because the goose was obviously, someone.

The big cat ignored the pig, studied the horses and cows who continued to quietly graze, turning, she continued toward the silo. Just then the kittens burst from the field, saw the sow, and started running toward her. They stopped when their mama growled at them, then turned and galloped back to her. All of them entered the silo.

Wally worked his way on his belly back to the pines and whispered. "Now, cats."

The five cats began quietly backing down from the trees. They slunk off toward the northeast until they were behind the silo. Then they began to slink on their bellies across the clearing. The noise from Rocky River was a blessing to the Larsen animals and the sounds of crunching and growling cougar kittens from inside the silo also covered any sounds made by the cats.

Horses and cattle clipped the grass closer and closer to the silo, working their way across the clearing. The grass was sweet but no one could taste it. The livestock were struggling to overcome their normal flight instincts, partly by glancing at their companions, partly by their fear of Wally, and finally because they knew they must do this valiant thing. They were the prey and yet, they were stalking a predator. Once the cougar looked out and stared at the cows, the bull, and the horses, but then she disappeared back inside the darkness.

After what seemed like an hour, but was only a few minutes, the silo was partially surrounded by three cows, one young bull, two horses and a large, white pig. Five little cats squatted in the dark, east of the silo, about ten feet away from its side. They lay flattened in the grass, listening to the terrible eating sounds coming from inside the silo and waiting for Wally's orders.

Wally, meanwhile, had crept on his belly across the clearing behind the horses and cows. The evening light was almost gone and even the long shadows from the animals were fading. It was time. Suddenly Wally sprang up and barked as loudly, and as angrily, as he could at the silo opening while calling at the same time, "Brawny, Brawny!"

The cougar snarled and tried to escape out of the opening, but Wally charged forward as he barked and he was too close by then. His fangs and barking backed her again into the darkness of the silo where she screamed her anger at him. In two bounds, the big bull charged the silo and barred the opening. Wally stayed at his side barking loudly. The sow drew close and started grunting at the north side of the silo while the cows came up behind the bull and began to moo as loudly as they could.

Brawny bawled, and pawed the ground, and swung his head back and forth in the most menacing way. The horses also stood on the north side of the bull and neighed loudly. They reared and stomped the ground, and then whirled and thumped the side of the silo with their hoofs.

Meanwhile, the cats had raced the last few feet and scampered up the rough sides of the silo until they were all on the roof. From there they yowled loudly into the vent openings. The snarls and screams coming from inside the silo were deafening, but the big cat made no attempt to run out because the bull and the dog barred the opening. The farm animals could hear her kittens screaming and crying to their mother for protection.

"Do you see that broken door hanging there?" Wally shouted to Brawny above the din.

"Yah," the bellow came back.

"See if you can push it with your horns to cover the exit."

"Dog, I gotta get close for that. My nose. My beautiful nose!"

"Remember the Larsens, you ugly piece of beef!"

The bull responded with loud bawls, a mixture of displeasure, anger, and fear, and yet he moved closer and managed to hook the door with one of his horns. It was a heavy door and it lay up against the silo still attached by one very old, long hinge. Brawny pulled at the door, the mama cougar inside snarled and screamed and reached out with one paw in an attempt to claw him, but the door gradually covered the opening and the vicious cougar could not reach the bull's face.

Wally stayed just a few feet out of range and continued his loud barking and ferocious growls with bared fangs and the ruff of his shoulder hair extended. It made him look bigger than he was.

"Back, cat! Back, killer! It's all over for you! Stay in there!" He roared in the most frightening way and the cats up on the roof were just as afraid of the dog, at that point, as they were of the cougar.

Then Trump moved closer and neighed to the bull, "Bull, let an old horse help you."

He lowered his head and pushed the side of the door with his forehead while Brawny, with one horn still hooked in a face board, backed up and pulled. Together the two managed to lift and push the door over the last part of the opening.

The rest of the animals continued snarling, meowing, grunting, mooing, and whinnying as Brawny lowered his head one more time. He hooked a lower crossbar of the door with a horn and lifted the entire door into place just as the cougar shot her paw out of the side. She screamed when the door slammed into her paw and jerked it back into the silo.

Trump stood back in admiration as Brawny then put his forehead against the door to hold it in place. The bull stood quietly, his sides heaving from the effort and from the adrenalin rushing through him.

"Well done, Brawny," Trump snorted to his companion. "I'll plow a furrow with you any day, my friend."

"Lady! Come here." Wally barked loudly, and the pig quickly trotted up to him. "Yes, you'll do just fine. Here, Lady, turn around now and sit down against the door."

Lady didn't bat an eyelash but simply obeyed the collie and backed her big seven hundred pound butt into the door and sat down.

Brawny bawled one more time and lifted his head from the door.

"And you too, Brawny."

"Aw-wah! I'm a bull, not a doorstop like bacon butt."

Wally looked at Brawny and didn't say anything. He just lowered his head and growled one more time, showing all of his teeth.

"Okay! Okay! You don't have to be like that. I'll do it." Brawny showed the whites of his eyes, then turned around and placed his butt against the door. He backed up and stiffened his front legs. As he did, he spoke to the sow for the very first time though they had been able to see each other from their respective pens for many months.

"Hitch over a bit, sis. We're cougar doorstops now." She slid over, the silo door creaked, the cougar snarled, and Brawny backed up a little bit more, pushing his big rump firmly against the heavy center cross bars of the door. It was done.

The cows came closer and bawled in relief. They were no longer as afraid although they still snorted and stiffened their front legs when they heard the snarls of the cougars inside. "Well, girls," Melody, the oldest cow drawled with a tremble in her voice, "there's a handsome bull with his butt against the door and his back to the evil thing. He makes a mighty fine figure, don't you think?"

Up on the silo roof Pounce shouted in amazement. "I got it, Catcher! I got it! I understood the cow talk!" He yowled with delight and the other cats laughed with him. Sitting on top of a silo filled with cougars, Pounce was at last a farm cat. He understood cow.

The cows also laughed in delight when Pounce shouted down again that he understood them. Then they continued to giggle in relief because the fearful thing was caged and, taking their cue from Melody, they began to bat their eyelashes at the young bull. The cougar was locked in the silo, held there by the pig and the bull. For the first time since Wally told them the plan, they felt safe.

"Oh, straw," Brawny complained.

"What?" Wally barked in concern.

"Nothing. It's just the cows. Can't you see they like me? How long I gotta stay here? Can a cougar dig a hole in this door and bite or claw me?"

Wally relaxed somewhat and sat down. His ruff settled but not completely. "Just wait, big hoofer. After a while we'll be able to go home. And after another little while, you and those big-eyed bovines will spend lots of time together."

The snarling inside gradually grew quiet and no other noise came from the silo except for an occasional thump. Big Yellow called down from the silo roof. "Wally, those kittens is nursing the cougar now. We sees them through the vents."

Even while clinging to the silo roof Catcher couldn't help herself and replied, "Are nursing. They are nursing."

"Yeah, yeah. That's what I sees down those vents, those kittens is nursing."

Catcher sighed and contented herself by planning a school for the cats when things were back to normal. Blackie understood and grinned at Catcher. She spoke poorly also, but the difference was that Blackie knew it, and the Yellow Boys did not.

It was dark and the air was cooling down some making everyone relax just a little bit. Wally flopped down on the ground. "Cats. You alright up there for now?"

Pounce spoke for them all. "It's not real comfortable, sir. But yes. We are fine for now."

"Well, troop. This is the way it is. Matthew and Bonny must

be home by now. They'll have discovered that we are all missing. Matthew will see your rope was chewed, Brawny. He'll wonder about it but think I did it to let you escape. And, he'll be right about that. Then he'll think something terrible has happened to all of us. He will have noticed that the pigpen door was pushed in. There's just one thing left for us to do and that is to wait for human help."

The cows were tired. It had been a long, exciting, and frightening day. They wanted to be milked. Their full utters were beginning to hurt and they mooed to go home. They missed their big calves and wanted to nurse them too, for Matthew never milked them dry but let the calves still nurse some every night.

Wally smiled at them. "Please, girls, stay here. You shouldn't walk along the river in the dark alone, and Brawny has to stay here to keep the cougar caged. So he can't take you home yet."

Brawny straightened up and lifted his head. His lyre shaped horns began to glint in the moonlight and his eyes seemed to sparkle as he gazed back at the cows, *his cows*. The girls decided that maybe they could wait just a little while longer after all. A young handsome bull in the field with them was very nice, even if he was holding a door closed with his butt, a very un-bull-like thing to do. They returned to giggling among themselves, then lay down and chewed their cuds, and tried not to think of their swollen and hurting udders.

"Lady, we owe you a great debt. You led into the clearing and faced the cougar first. All of us thank you." Wally nodded to the pig as he spoke. It confused the animals but because it was Wally doing the nodding, all the animals nodded to her. The cats couldn't see the pig very well from their silo perch but they remained respectfully silent.

Lady began to speak quietly, and Pounce was pleased to hear the melody in her voice. It made him wonder if she had a poetic soul. *I must talk to her later*, he thought.

"I know we're just bacon to most of you, but it is the truth and we are okay with it. We are bacon." She spoke without any malice or defense. "Thank you, Wally." She turned and nodded toward the collie. "I'm happy you asked me to participate in this great adventure to help restore the whole farm to Matthew and Bonny. It is the right thing to do. Pigs know how things are for we are very smart, though it doesn't look smart to root in the mud and to accept being bacon. Yet, there is an order to things and people are in charge of those things and not us. Each year my piglets are taken away from me. They go far away. That is the way of things and we pigs accept the way of things."

Lady paused and shifted her weight a bit before continuing. "The way of things is to do what is right, when it is right. It is right that our people own their farms and that the wild things do not own them. It is right that we live with people and the wild things do not. It is right that we did what we normally don't do so that the wild things have to stop doing what they should not do. Pigs know the way of things, so I am honored to be included in non-pig-like work with those of you who are not pig-like."

Pounce could hardly constrain himself. He could hear the poetry in her speech. Her lines, *the way of things* and *non-pig-like*, almost prompted him to rhapsodize while he clung to the silo roof with the other four cats. Instead, he contented himself with internal hums and with repeating her phrasing. He didn't want to forget the beauty of what she said, though he wasn't sure what the whole speech meant. Nevertheless, he made a right turn in his little cathead upon the top of a silo filled with cougars. He was a cat who liked pigs and it only took a second to make up his mind. His mama had been right. *It doesn't matter where you are or what your circumstances are when it's time to think right about something; that is, to change your mind. Just do it.*

Pounce squatted and mused on his mother's words and started humming a little "I like pigs" song, but when Wally began speaking, Pounce's song floated away and was forgotten.

"It was a Pounce idea, Lady." Wally sighed and spoke slowly and it was plain that he was tired and showing his age. "Pounce is one of us now. He has shown his loyalty to our family. If he had not boldly spoken his plan, if he had remained in the dog-cat order of things, we would not have today's victory."

The cows and horses looked up at Pounce on top of the silo as the other cats looked on in wonder. Those were amazing words coming from Wally and they all knew it. Moonlight silhouetted all the crouching cats on the silo, but the white fur on the little black and white cat seemed to glisten in the moonlight.

Then Wally did the unthinkable. He bowed to a cat, the Pounce cat. The animals gasped with the knowledge of its implication. The order of things, at least on this day, had indeed turned upside down. Before another second could pass, the cows kneeling on the grass lowered their noses to the ground, and the big horses each put one leg forward and lowered their heads on it. Brawny and Lady also, who could not see the cats on the silo, lowered their heads in wonder.

Everyone was quiet and pondering what it all meant, but Pounce wasn't thinking *order of thing* thoughts at all. He was simply embarrassed. "Ah, you guys. It wasn't anything. I just got mad at the cougar. That's all."

Catcher moved closer to him. "Wasn't anything? Pounce, the most vicious wild beast in these parts is trapped in the silo and it's not anything?"

She reached forward suddenly and licked him right across his nose between his whiskers. He nearly fell off the silo in surprise but Catcher grabbed one of his ears in her teeth to help him regain his balance, and that made all the cats laugh. Then every animal grew quiet and settled down to wait.

The silo was silent.

11

Rescue and Removal

Through the night a distant sound became a roar coming toward them, followed by bouncing trucks. Down the overgrown farm road that led in from the east came Matthew's truck, followed by Fred Benson's truck, followed by Ableforth's truck with Dwight Ableforth and Leo Swensen in it. Headlights flooded the area as the vehicles spread out around the animals. In an instant Matthew was out of his truck carrying a rifle and running toward the animals.

Wally rushed toward him and blocked his way. "Matthew," he barked. "Slow down. We got them."

The men gathered alongside Matthew. They tried to take in the scene. They saw the sow sitting against the lower part of the silo door. Next to her stood the big bull with his butt pushed into the crossbars and his front legs stiffened. The three cows lying down in front of them were calmly chewing their cud. Off to the north of them the horses were grazing as though nothing was out of order. A slight movement on top of the silo grabbed their attention. Raising their flashlights, they saw the shine from the eyes of five cats squatting on the silo roof, blinking back into the beams.

The sound of thrashing and several thumps suddenly erupted

from within the silo, followed by the scream of the big cat and the snarls of her kittens. Cautiously Matthew walked forward as Wally slowly backed up and partially blocked his way. Reaching the silo, Matthew looked through a crack and began to shout. "I don't believe it! Guys! Look at this!" Matthew was beside himself.

It was right that Matthew's closest neighbors should be the first men to find out that the cougar, the county menace, had been captured. Fred Benson was Matthew's nearest neighbor to the north. Leo Svensen, the dairy farmer, had his spread southwest of the Larsen farm along an original rural route through the farmlands and Dwight Ableforth, the nursery owner and chicken farmer, was located west of Leo along the old highway just past the bridge that crossed Rocky River in front of the Larsen farm.

These mature men were Matthew's dearest and closest friends from his childhood. They were descendants of the original homesteaders, and now they walked around the silo carefully, carrying their rifles. Wally grinned and sighed in pleasure. The farms of these men had been passed down to them from their fathers, just as Matthew's had. They loved the land and their animals just as much as Matthew did. Wally knew these men, their farms, and their farm dogs.

It was a grand feeling the old collie had, and he wished he could share it with a few of his dog friends like Ableforth's terrier-mix, Happy, and Svensen's cowdogs, the beautiful Border Collie bitches, Callie and Ginger. He knew he would get to see Fred Benson's Australian Shepherd dog, Banger, soon because Fred and his wife often had the dog with them when they stopped to visit.

Yet, of all his friends, Wally longed to share this day's story with Old Pharoah, the great German Shepherd living on the farm to the east of them. Old Pharoah and Wally had a unique bond and shared experiences, and Wally determined in his warm dog's heart to remember all the details of this adventure to share with him the next time they met.

None of the animals moved as the men hurried by them. The horses kept cropping grass in front of the barn and the cows kept chewing as the men passed. They acted as though these events were normal. Wally was suddenly amused, remembering how these same cows had to close their eyes earlier, lest the sight of the cougar should send them into a panic. Wally was sure they would be much calmer cows from now on. And even the brave horses had gained more courage.

The men moved forward carrying their rifles. Peering inside through the small cracks and using their flashlights, they saw the cougar crouched and cornered. She and her half-grown kittens snarled back at the lights with eyes filled with hatred and fear. Matthew roared back, but it was directed to the men.

"Well, fellows, we gotta a problem and I don't think it can be solved safely until daylight, and I see if our Fish and Game guys will come out here in the mornin' too."

Fred Benson answered. "Let's use whatever we have to secure the door and then help Matthew get the animals home."

"Yeah, yeah." Leo Svensen the dairy farmer studied the Randall cows. "Dim cows got dim big utters in needs of milkin' right off. Veel help ya, Matt-chew. Veel help ya take dim pretty cows home."

The men went to their trucks and returned with ropes and chains that they used to secure the silo. Afterward, Matthew grabbed the chewed rope hanging from Brawny's halter and pulled. The big bull moved forward, following him without looking back. It felt so good to bend his knees normally again.

Wally barked at Lady. "It's done, Lady. Good girl. Couldn't have done it without you. Follow Brawny home now." She stood up and walked stiffly after the bull.

"Come on down, cats. Time to go home." Wally yapped happily up to the silo roof felines. The cats hurried down backwards, their claws digging into the wood of the aged pine boards. "What a day, gang. What a day." Wally stretched and yawned as he walked over to the Morgan horses. "Fellows, we'll talk tomorrow. Good job, men. Good job." Wally nosed the horses in a quiet thank you.

The animals seemed content with whatever would happen next as Matthew went to his truck. Rummaging behind the seat, Matthew found a couple of halters and ropes, and an extra length of rope for Brawny. The loud man murmured as he stroked the horses' faces while haltering them.

"Oh, guys. You had me worried." Then the big man did something very Pounce-like though it was something uncharacteristic for him. He kissed the noses of his horses without caring whether the other farmers saw him or not. Dwight turned away, Fred brushed his eyes, and Leo pulled his big red handkerchief from his overalls and blew his nose loudly. They understood, without speaking, that the bond a man has with his animals tends to run very deep.

"I'm gettin' too old for this, men." Matthew laughed as he climbed into the back of his truck, and then hoisted himself over onto Trump's back. "Let's see now. Leo, why don't ya ride Spade? The cows will go wherever we go. They just want to go home. I'll lead the bull and the pig will follow him. Oh ya, my cats. Let's see. The black one and the yellow ones will make their way home. One of you guys, hand me the black and white one, and that pretty, gray-striped girl there."

Dwight handed Pounce to Matthew who tucked him under his right arm and on his hip with a little squeeze. "Hi, puss."

Fred had already picked up a very willing Catcher and was scratching her thoroughly. She almost leaped into Matthew's lap, so eager to go home. "Sit tight, girl," he said with a pat. He didn't know that she had already learned how to ride a horse earlier that day.

She leaned back into his flannel shirt and smelled the barn and the house and Bonnie and everything that meant home to her. She began to purr and was joined by Pounce's loud rumble. Matthew chuckled when he heard the contented chorus.

"Ha! So ya like bein' rescued, do ya?" He chuckled again as he picked up Trump's halter rope and the bull's rope together in his left hand. Turning the horse with knee pressure, he started for home.

The sow followed the bull. The cows followed the sow. Leo Svensen rode Spade behind them, followed by Fred and Dwight in their trucks. What a comical procession they made as they slowly filed out of the clearing and down the overgrown road toward the Larsen farm.

The Yellow Boys fussed about not getting to ride back, but Blackie reminded them that they had been lolling on top of a silo for hours and the walk would be good for them. They all decided they'd had enough of the river and the darkness and everything else so they trotted along behind Spade on the old road. Blackie was too tired to care that trucks with men in them were following her on the road. People seemed okay to her that night though she kept shooting glances over her shoulder.

After a bit, the three cats turned off the road and cut across the fields and arrived in the barnyard before the rest of the group. The walking cows and horses slowed the trucks following them, but the drivers didn't seem to mind. They knew animals, and they were perfectly willing to get home late. So they crept down the dirt road behind the slow moving, cougar-catching farm animals.

The road trip was a lot shorter than the trail by the river had been earlier, and the animals were glad since it had been a long day for everyone. Pounce and Catcher purred, and almost dozed as they rocked to the steady movement of the horse on the way home. The clip-clop of Trump's hooves was soothing, and the warm arms of the big, loud man were, indeed, the best place to be that night.

Sunday, the morning after the "silo business" as Bonny called it, the Larsens stayed home from church to wait for the men who also gave up their Sunday to come out and collect the cougars. Fred and the Fish and Game people were to arrive that morning fairly early, and though Matthew was overtired, he was itching to get back to the homestead and check on the cougars. Bonny listened to him mutter while quietly making a huge pot of coffee and setting out the sweet rolls she would serve the Fish and Game men when they arrived.

Charlie Danielson would be partnered with young Thomas Martin. Both men had grown up in the area. Matthew had known Charlie and his family for years. They had a small, five-acre place on the edge of town and Charlie's wife, Betsy, was a good friend to Bonny. Matthew called her Bonny's "pickle partner" because the women exchanged pickle recipes and entered the same contests at the fair together. They also saw her in church quite regularly though Charlie didn't attend.

Thomas, however, came from a city family that emphasized college education for all of their children though Matthew reckoned that more kids ought to learn trades. He also felt that a man fresh out of college, like young Thomas, should not hold such an important job with the Fish and Game department. It rankled him since he figured the job should have gone to one of the country people who, he thought, really understood country matters about wild game and such.

"They just don't know what farmers need, Bonny. They don't respect our rights. Always harpin' about fish rights, and bird rights, and snail rights, and owl rights, and cougar rights, and deer rights, and, and, and what about our rights? I speck a coyote's got more rights than a man nowadays!" This last salvo was delivered with more than Matthew's usual volume.

"You must let it go, dear. I'm sure they are following the law and doing their job. You know Charlie. He's our friend."

"Charlie is a man, Bonny. I trust him! But these kids they put in charge of our affairs. It's not right. No sir, it's just not right!"

"These kids, dear, as you call them, are well trained. Betsy tells me about the courses Charlie had to study years ago and Thomas had to study even more things ..."

"That's just it, Bonny. They study and study and study. Then they go out in the woods and put tags on everythin' that breathes. Then they come and tell us not to breathe, or to let our cows breathe because we might pollute somethin'! Why would a farmer pollute his own farm?" Matthew's roaring filled the house and kept Pounce cowering under the table. Even Wally sat with his head pushed back against the door in concern.

"Now, dear. Calm down. In a little bit the men will be here, and you will be nice to young Thomas. He knows the law better than Charlie."

"Yah. Helped make it no doubt!"

"Matthew!" Bonny spoke sharply, then lowered her voice. "Dear, the men are on their way. Let's have a pleasant visit and let them do their duty. Please?"

Matthew mumbled under his breath. "I should have gone back and shot the cougars and buried them where no one would know and then told everyone that they broke out and got away and, and ..."

Bonny smiled as his anger faded. She knew her man. He talked loud and big and angry sometimes, but he always obeyed the law and did what was right. That was her Matthew, an honest man.

The big Fish and Game truck crunched the yard gravel drawing Matthew and Bonny outside to greet the arrivals. Fred Benson arrived a few minutes later in his pickup truck. Then, in typical country fashion, Bonnie offered them a cup of hot coffee along with a plate of warm cinnamon rolls. How could they refuse? The talk was animated but Matthew and Fred were strangely silent about the cougar and cubs' capture and only talked about how they had chained up the silo with the beasts inside.

After the coffee and rolls, Matthew climbed up to ride with Fred. "Come on, Wall," Matthew yelled in his usual booming fashion. Wally did not need a second invitation but nimbly hopped into the back of Fred's pickup. Once out of the Larson drive, they turned down the old dirt track they had followed the night before. But this time their hearts were peaceful and not anxious. Fred led the authorities up the old road to the original homestead, and there they found it just as they had left it the night before.

The beautiful fields surrounding the old buildings were sparkling with health. The morning sun was beginning to dry the dew from the deep green grass while the noise from the river made the men talk louder as they surveyed the tranquil scene. Matthew's farm truck was still parked facing the silo. The chains on the silo were still tightly in place. Not a sound came from inside the silo. It did not look dangerous, but the men knew that the way things appear does not always reveal the way things are.

Cautiously they all stepped down from the trucks. Matthew held onto Wally's collar as Fred led slowly toward the silo. Wally begun a low, menacing growl and Charlie gripped a rifle. Suddenly, from inside the silo, rustlings and snarls and thumps erupted and the three cougars began to thrash around and claw at the silo. A large tawny paw shot out the only opening at the top left-hand corner of the busted door and then just as quickly pulled back in.

"Ha. There she is," Charlie shouted with glee. He waved the gun in the air and laughed. "Well, Matthew, you got them sure." He laughed even louder. "And trussed in pretty tight with chains and ropes, I see." Charlie walked back to the big truck and, turning it around, calmly backed it up to the silo. Meanwhile, Thomas peered in through the cracks and confirmed the presence of the three cougars.

"How'd you get them in there, Mr. Larson?" Thomas Martin asked.

Matthew studied the young agent in his smartly pressed official shirt, and his shiny boots before answering. "Actually, they were driven in there by my dog."

He had wisely decided not to tell the officials that five cats, two horses, three cows, a sow, a bull, and one old collie had done the deed. It was much too wild of a tale for ordinary people to believe. He might tell Charlie privately, but not yet. Fred grinned and turned his head away, not wanting to add anything to the story either.

Charlie climbed down from the truck cab carrying another rifle and a small case that he gave to Thomas. The farmers stood back and watched as Thomas deftly prepared to shoot darts into the cougars.

"We'll just shoot through a crack here and put her down," he said as he walked up to the silo. "It won't hurt her."

He made that last remark for the farmers, but he could have saved his breath. Both Matthew and Fred remembered cattle in the county that had been lost to cougars, years before. There was no love in the men for big cats that chose to live in farming country. Fred was especially angry and silent. His eyes were as narrow as the thin cracks in the silo walls he had peeked through, for in the daylight, he recognized the spotted remains of his missing prize goat.

A popping sound and a deep snarl was followed by a bit of thrashing. A minute or so later the big cat was down as her kittens snarled and whined beside her. Thomas Martin spoke quickly as he prepared to shoot the cubs. "I really hate to dart the cubs but they are pretty big and could hurt one of us. We'll give them just a little dose and maybe that will be enough."

"This will wear off fairly quickly so let's get it done," Charlie added after the two cubs were darted.

The men briskly removed the chains and ropes. It took two of them to lift the broken door away from the opening. After a lot of grunting, the door fell away with a loud crash and this time the last hinge broke off. "How in the world did you get that heavy thing up here in the first place?" Charlie asked.

Matthew just shrugged and muttered, "Teamwork."

Fred grinned again and kept his head down while helping drag out the cubs. They measured them, checked their general health, and put them in one of the cages. Wally meanwhile sniffed and growled and walked around in charge of all goings-on. He stuck his nose into the big cat's fur when the men pulled her out of the silo. He would have bitten down to help Matthew drag her, but was stopped with a loud command. "Down, Wall! Out of the way!"

Handling the big heavy cat took longer. After measuring and examining her carefully, all four men lifted her into the truck and closed her up in a large cage. "She appears perfectly healthy, Matthew," Charlie commented. "Looks like she chose to live in our county rather than hunt wild game where she came from."

Matthew stepped forward when the men were finished and all three cats were caged.

"How far away will you take them before they're released? In the hills here?"

"No, sir. Not in these hills," Thomas Martin replied. "This female cougar would just come back. She's been here a while and found it easy pickings. And her youngsters only know farm hunting. These animals will no doubt be placed in a national park a very long way from here. It's not our decision, but regardless of where it's determined to place them, it's unlikely you'll ever see this big girl again."

Matthew suddenly felt a little better toward young Thomas. After handshakes all around, the Fish and Game men left with their cargo of sleepy big cats. A wonderful sense of relief settled over Matthew and Fred as they watched the authorities leave and even Wally flopped down on the ground and rolled over on his back with a big sigh. It was over.

CHAPTER 12

Teamwork

The morning went quickly as Matthew and Fred spent time examining the silo and the partially fallen buildings. "You know, Matthew, I think a work party is in order here. I'll get the boys and we'll come over some day and knock all this down if you're a-willing. It's the least we can do after what your 'team' did for all of us." At this, Fred broke down and laughed and laughed. It was a man-sized belly laugh, and it helped wash the tension away as Matthew joined in with his normal bellow.

"Come on, Fred. Let's get the ladies and take 'em to town for a nice Sunday afternoon dinner. Today we ain't farmers. We're city slickers on the town with our women."

After deciding when and where to meet, they climbed into their trucks and set out. Wally sat on the seat with Matthew, pleased and relieved that their plan had worked.

He could hardly wait to get home and tell the other animals how the big cats had been darted and then dragged into cages. Thinking about it made the big collie grin even wider on the bumpy ride home.

"Good boy, Wall. I don't know how you fellas did all that, but good boy. We were wonderin' where she had holed up, and completely missed checkin' out the silo. I should have guessed that was why the cows and horses stayed in the home fields. Good boy." All this was said as one giant hand pounded a broad collie back while they bumped along home.

The rest of the day was filled with cats and cows and horses, and a sow, listening to the story of how the cougars were caged and trucked away. They begged for it over and over until Wally finally refused to tell it again. Then the cats went back to mouse chasing and rolling in the straw and other pussycat activities. The horses galloped around their pasture and kicked up their heels and even the cows, whose big calves were with them in the pasture for the day, ran around a bit too. Playtime helped to wash away the tension all the animals had been under.

Lady was content to lie in her pen and dream while her piglets nosed around in their pen next to her, and Brawny lay quietly on a pile of straw in his corral, dozing the afternoon away. Lady's pen and Brawny's corral had hastily constructed temporary poles jammed here and there and the animals could have pushed their way out, but this Sunday they were content to stay in the places made for them. Their spirit for adventure had been fully satisfied the day before and all they wanted now was the comfortable and the familiar surroundings of home.

Just past midday Matthew and Bonny went to town for that special dinner with Fred and Sally. Bonny lost no time getting ready for the trip, secretly hoping that Matthew's good mood would extend to an hour of shopping after dinner. She hoped to coax him into trying on some new clothes. *That man,* she thought, *walks around in rags and won't buy anything new to wear.* Of course, she already knew from her friends that most of the other farmers were as uninterested in what the ladies called "decent clothes" as her Matthew. Smiling and hopeful, short and round, Bonny climbed into the truck as Matthew roared at her.

"Bonny! Gonna take all day? Come on, lady. Your man's a-starvin'." His eyes twinkled at her and she smiled.

"I love you, you loud thing, you," she replied while pulling her roundness up into the truck.

"Ha, ha," roared the loud thing as he turned down the drive and headed toward Ablesforth Crossing and fellowship with two dear friends.

Like the guard he was, Wally sat at the head of the pasture on the rise just before the Larson driveway entered the main road. From there he usually could see the cows and horses grazing in their field, unless they went down around the south bend by the bridge. Though Wally stayed home with them, none of the animals felt the need for a guard. The cougar was gone and they were giddy with delight. Not one of them remembered that their countryside was still home to raccoons, and coyotes, and birds of prey, and foxes, and occasionally a feral dog or two. Only Wally remembered, smiled at their antics, and kept watch.

By early afternoon Lady was rested from the exertion of the previous day and seemed more animated as she rooted around in her pen. Every grunt and snort sounded musical for she seemed to have written a song. It was a rare pig poem from a happy pig. She had been useful to her people and it made her content.

> "A pig helped catch a cougar, sugar,
> The bacon saved the day.
> A pig's butt held the door in place,
> 'Til they took the beast away.
> Hey! Hey!
> A pig's butt held the door in place,
> 'Til they took the beast away.
> Hey! Hey!"

Although she sang so low with her snout in the dirt that it was somewhat hard to catch all of the words, Pounce heard them clearly. He stood outside her pen waving his tail in the air to the solid beat of her poem. When she finished her song and once more sank down on the moist ground to doze, Pounce went away humming, "Hey! Hey! Hey! Hey!"

He went into the barn and began to leap among the straw bales and run up and down in front of the stalls. He yodeled with delight and meowed loudly. Then he walked sideways and chased shadows on the walls and sang to himself and anyone else who wanted to listen. It was more than the happy song of a fearless cat because a deadly threat was gone. Something else had turned the music up a notch in Pounce.

The Yellow Boys lolled on the top rail of the calf pen and watched Pounce with amusement. Even the calves had moved up to the barn and were listening to the cat with interest. The Morgan horses only looked up once in a while from their grazing in the field, and the cows chewed their cuds without seeming to listen or to look. A cat yodeling in the barn seemed somehow normal to them. However, if cows grin while chewing, then there was a bit of extra movement around their mouths when the sound of yodeling blew out over the pasture.

"Lookie, lookie, bro. Kiddle Pounce is losing it." Little Yellow stared intently at Pounce and wondered.

"Yeah, son. But ain't love grand?" Both yellow cats sat upright on the top rail of the calves' pen and began boxing each other with their front paws as Pounce continued to sing.

"I'm dancing and prancing for Catcher's romancing
Will keep me on dancing around,
Purr-round, purr-round,
Will keep me on dancing around."

Catcher lay on a straw bale and giggled while Pounce leaped around singing. He was a tightly wound little spring and couldn't seem to stop. Finally, after singing his song through three complete times, he leaped up on the straw bale and fell beside her.

"Aw, Pounce, you silly thing." She grinned as she reached out to lick the tip of one of his ears.

He licked one of her ears in return, and then decided to give her a serious wash. He had just started on the patch of hair between Catcher's ears when he suddenly sat up.

"Oh, no."

"What?"

"The question, Catcher, is what now? Do we live in the barn together or in the house together? What do you think Matthew and Bonny will allow?"

"Well," Catcher answered slowly. "I suppose we will wait and find out. We are cats, you know, and we can be verrrry patient." Catcher held on to the word "very" and trilled it through her teeth so that the "r's" rolled.

Pounce laughed. "You're right, of course. Whatever they decide will be fine with me. But I do hope they decide on the house. Chicken gravy you know and warm beds at night and ..." His voice trailed off as he caught sight of Blackie coming down the barn aisle.

"I hope your dopy song didn't wake my kits," she scolded. Her tone of voice was friendly and the other cats knew it. She leaped up lightly and walked along the edge of their bale and spoke again before dropping down the kitten hole. "I hope youse sappy cats will be very happy cats."

"Thank you, Blackie," Pounce and Catcher said together.

"Duh, Pouncer is in love, little lady, and the Catcher is too, I t'ink." Little Yellow mocked playfully as he pursed his lips in a kissing fashion. "Smack, smack," his lips sang.

"Yes, boys. Pounce is my choice. We will be very happy, I am sure of it."

"No offence, Catcher." Big Yellow answered as he stood up and stretched. "The kid here is a little quick to meow what he thinks, before he thinks." Big Yellow glared at his younger brother, although Little Yellow was only younger by a few minutes.

Pounce stood and stretched also and then answered. "It's alright, fellows. I've done my share of meowing too. And no offense is taken by either of us."

Catcher smiled at Pounce. It pleased her that he had spoken for both of them and had not become offended for her sake. It showed her that he was maturing into an adult cat. She rubbed her shoulder against his. "I heard the pickup. They're home. Let's go."

They waved their tails at the other cats as they jumped down from the straw bales and hurried out of the tool and straw room. They rounded the corner into the main barn aisle, out of sight of the other cats, before Catcher spoke. "I thought if we went toward the house together, Matthew and Bonny would see us and perhaps they might, you know …"

Her voice trailed off with Pounce's interruption. "Ha. I love that about you. Always thinking. Good girl. Let's go." Pounce quickened his pace as his mind leaped ahead to wonder what Bonny was cooking for supper. Then he remembered that they had gone somewhere else to eat. That seemed strange to Pounce since there were always so many good things to eat in Bonny's kitchen already. As they approached the door, Catcher began to hang back.

"It's been a while since I've been in the house. I don't …"

"No, you don't. Your idea is a great one and we won't know unless we try. I heard Bonny tell Matthew just a couple of days ago, 'You have not because you ask not.'" Pounce spoke firmly as he stared into Catcher's deep green eyes.

"What does that mean?"

"Well, she was reading out of that book they take when they go to church. So I guess it is something important to them. I'm not sure, but I am sure of this. Bonny always gives me food or petting when I ask her for it. So let's just ask. Okay?"

Catcher stopped on the mat outside the front door. She sat down before she answered.

"Okay, Pounce. Okay."

With that, Pounce stood up on his hind legs and patted the door with his front feet, at the same time he called to Bonny. "Purr-ounce! Purr-ounce!"

A chair scraped against the floor inside and the cats listened as quick footsteps came to the door. "Pounce, you rascal. I was looking for you. Didn't you hear me calling?"

Bonny was talking to him even before she opened the door. Instantly the black and white cat was rubbing his body against her leg. "Come on, Catcher. Get the other leg before she moves."

Then the silver stripped beauty began working her length against Bonny's other leg. Both cats looking longingly up into Bonny's face and purred with all their might.

"Well, well, you two. What are you up to tonight?"

Before they could answer with meows or purrs, Bonny bent over and scooped both cats up into her arms. Turning back into the house, she closed the door behind her with a kick from one foot and continued over to the chairs by the window. Plopping both cats in her own chair she backed up and sat down in the other. "Okay. 'Fess up. What have you two been up to? Mischief, no doubt."

Both cats lay right where she put them, but rolled over onto their backs and showed one white and one gray belly between them. From upside down, they blinked their eyes in cat smiles and purred as loudly as they could, and reached their front legs towards Bonny.

"Aw, Pounce, you rascal. You've got a girlfriend, right? And Catcher, I've missed you. I didn't think you wanted to be at the house any more."

Two stretching and loudly purring cats wiggled upside down in front of her and then rubbed their noses against her hand when she reached out to pet them.

"I know Matthew wants you down in the barn at night. But with Blackie and the Yellow Boys there, I don't think any more cats are needed to protect the grain. Do you?"

By this time Bonny was on her knees in front of the cats. She cuddled their heads in her hands and rubbed their front paws against her cheeks. Pounce soaked up the attention, but found his mind wondering a bit. There was something on top of the stove, and it smelled awfully good. He started swinging his head in that direction.

"Ha, boy. You're full of beans. I see your nose going to the pot on the stove. That's mama's best leftover stew. I was warming it up just for you. You watch. Although Matthew ate a big steak in town, I bet he'll have a bit of your stew anyway. Ha." Bonny left the cats, washed her hands and then returned to stir the little stew pot on the stove. After the table was set and two little dishes were placed on the sideboard for the cats, she sat down in Matthew's chair and considered the cats.

"I suppose you will be trying to win over Matthew tonight. Well, I don't know. He's kind of stuck in his ways you know, cats in the barn and all of that. But today he bought some new shirts and pants. The old farmer is shaping up right nice." Bonny chuckled with pleasure, and her round frame seemed to chuckle right along with her. "We'll see. But you let me do the talking and stay out of his way. That business at the silo may help some, but I'm not promising. I'm not promising anything. I just don't know."

The cats settled down to wait on Bonny's chair and after grooming each other, they gradually fell into an easy sleep. They didn't know how she would do it, but after the head rubbing and paw pulling and belly scratching and little kisses between their ears, both cats were sure Bonny would do something grand.

Pounce jerked and twitched as he slept. He was chasing a pot full of stew that seemed to keep moving just a little ahead of him. Catcher was especially relaxed and content. As she drifted into sleep, she sang to herself, Pounce-like.

"She wants me, she loves me ... of this I'm sure.
She wants me, she loves me ... purr, purr, purr."

CHAPTER 13

Work Party Friends

The following Saturday, early in the morning, neighbors showed up along with some of the families from Peace Lutheran Church. Bonny was glad to see her friends from their church as well as her dear and near neighbors. The women brought baskets of fresh bread, bowls of salads, platters of fried chicken, and homemade sausages. Men came with tools to use in tearing down the old buildings.

It was all very exciting for the animals on the Larsen farm. Chickens ran through the lawn in front of the house because Bonny, in her excitement, had forgotten to close the chicken house door that morning after gathering the eggs. She knew that Wally would help her round them up later. So she just kept saying, "Shoo, shoo," and hoped the birds would not get in the way too much.

From time to time Brawny bellowed to the cows. He had taken a special interest in them now that they were better acquainted and it looked like the cows returned his interest. The speckled ladies didn't want to go down to the river and graze that morning. Instead, they stayed in the pasture nearest the barn and Brawny's corral. Matthew had noted their attention to one another, and addressed his bull while feeding him.

"Soon, big fellow. You and the girls will have the field by the river and the fields up at the old homestead too. After the last ha-yin' is over, you'll have the pastures on the eastside too. Speakin' of which, I've got to speak to the Andersen brothers today about that job."

Matthew stopped scratching Brawny's face and pondered the various needs coming up. He had stopped cutting his own hay several years previously and hired the Anderson brothers instead. A few of his older neighbors, like himself, were doing the same. It had become cost effective to hire the job done, put up the hay needed, and sell the rest. In fact, for several years Matthew's hay sales had exceeded his expectations and had added a little more cash to the Larsen farm operation. Brawny wasn't sure what Matthew meant when he talked, but he loved the head rubbing so he pushed his huge head against Matthew for more.

"Okay, beefsteak! That's enough!" Matthew laughed, backed out of Brawny's pen, closed the new, extra heavy gate and thought, *now that was a good investment!* He studied the stronger poles and gate that had cost him several days of huffing and puff-ing to build and grinned with pleasure.

"Old Brownie was a wimp compared to you, bully-boy," Matthew hollered at his bull as he walked away and joined the men around their trucks.

The big boys were going with the men to help on the home-stead so there wasn't much for the half-grown boys to do and they didn't want to play with the girls. But Matthew understood boys and so just before he, the men, and teenage boys left that morning, he gave Leo Svensen's grandsons, Little Leo and Henry, eight and nine years old respectively, halters and lead ropes for the horses.

"You young men take the little ones for rides around the pas-ture and don't trot. Just walk the horses. You understand me?" He roared the instructions into their eager, upturned faces.

"Yes, sir," they chorused, grinning from ear to ear. This was a special treat for little Leo and his brother Henry. Their farm had a tractor and a small loader, but Matthew Larsen had the Morgan horses! Everyone in the county admired these beautiful animals that had won trotting races and pulling contests for years at the county fair. Trump was also the father of a number of good Morgan colts and fillies all over the state.

Leo Svenson, the boys' father Carl, and the boys' older teen-age brothers William and Johnny watched the young boys in their family haltering the magnificent Morgan horses by the barn as they drove away with the rest of the men. All the men were grinning.

Pulling down the buildings on the old homestead took the entire morning. The rotted logs and boards of the old barn came tumbling down easily, but the house required more work to take apart; in fact, most of the men worked all morning to take it down because they tried to save many of the handmade hardwood pieces.

Several of the men working that day were rural farmers with school-age children in their homes. Even though they all had known a cougar was in the nearby hills, it had been shocking news to these fathers that cougars were actually hunting so close to their homes and families. They shook away the images of their children standing alone waiting for school buses while cougars roamed the nearby fields.

Now the cougars were gone and the fathers, both the church-going ones and those who were not, worked with relief in their hearts and thanksgiving too. They tore into the old silo with relish. It was hard, dirty, fulfilling work as they finished this business of destroying the cougar's den. The men hooked heavy cables to the silo where the large iron rings surrounded it, cut through exactly the right posts, and then as the old silo creaked, they pulled it over with Ralph Schmidt's flatbed delivery truck. All the men shouted and cheered as it fell in a great cloud of dust and debris.

While that was taking place, Reverend Arden Bergstrum and

Dwight Ableforth walked over the clearing carefully. They were looking for a boarded-up well which would be dangerous for grazing animals. Instead they found a small, rotting landing at the river, tucked up under the trees leaning out over the water. They figured that the original homestead had gotten its water from the river and that meant no holes had been dug in the ground. This was good news because safely closing up an old well could be both time-consuming and dangerous work.

The old outhouse behind the house on the field's edge was another matter. It would have to be filled in. Matthew and Leo Svensen ran a chain around the middle of it and dragged it off its base using a pick-up truck. It fell over as it was being pulled. Peering down into the hole they saw that it was shallow and would not take much filling.

"I'll bring my little cat over after dis debris is picked up, Matt-chew. Veel 'ave dis 'ole filled in right quick. Then veel level this old place and make it fit for dim pretty cows. Juul see." Leo spoke cheerfully in his thick accent as he slapped Matthew's back.

When they stopped in mid morning to drink coffee out of thermoses and eat Bonny's sweet rolls, Matthew told the men what he'd do next. "Guys, I'll call The Cole Company to brin' their loader and dump trucks out for the cleanup. So don't ya'll worry about anythin' more. Cows and horses gonna graze where cougars once walked."

This was said in Matthew's usual booming style. The men hollered, the religious among them said amen, and a couple of men offered mild curses in agreement. All in all, it was a satisfied group of men and teenage boys drinking coffee and doing the male bonding thing around heaps of rotten lumber, rusty iron, and other debris.

Before they started the job, Matthew told the men to save the original windows and frames from the house and barn if they could. Bonny had asked for them, and he knew that those old glass panes and antique frames would make her happy though

he could not fathom why she wanted them. Other than old harnesses, Matthew liked new stuff and keeping things from the past
or displaying them in specialty stores, like the fashion was now,
made the farmer shake his head in disbelief. *Why people had even
come to their door asking if they had any antiques to sell. What is the
world coming to?* So Matthew pondered the strangeness of people's
choices and yet saved any old thing his beloved Bonny desired.

The men saved as many of the good pieces of hand-hewn
hardwood for Matthew as they could, including a fireplace mantel and wood from the window ledges in both the house and the
barn. Bonny had reminded Matthew that his great grandfather
had made them and she was sure Matthew could find a use for
them on the farm. His head began to fill with ideas of things he
could make for Bonny. *Perhaps even that porch swing she's been beg-
gin' me for, or the bench she wants just outside the kitchen door.* His
hands itched to examine the hardwood pieces more closely and
begin planning their use. *The remains of the past might be built into
somethin' useful for the future. Ah, Bonny.*

These thoughts would have to wait for the men were saying
that they would come back to finish the job they had started.
Matthew came back from his mental trip in time to hear that
they wanted to check fences and gates and refurbish gates with
new hardware where needed.

Ralph Schmidt spoke. "After the Coles come out, I'll bring
my boys and come back and use building magnets to search for
nails, or wire bits, and then we'll do a good hand raking of the
area. We'll pick up anything that can harm the animals when
they graze here."

"Ah, guys, I'll do the finish up around here," Matthew grunted back.

"Hey, the boys will love doing this. It will be an adventure for
them. Come on now. We want to do this." Ralph spoke quickly
and raised his voice as he always did when he would not be de-
nied. All the men knew by his quickness of speech that rejecting

his offer was not possible. Ralph's strong, round face was set and he could raise his voice almost as loud as Matthew could. He also owned Ableforth Crossing's only lumberyard and hardware store. If anyone could find every scrap of wire and hidden nail in the ground, it would be Ralph.

"We need to dig out the iron that circled the silo. Those rusty hoops will make fantastic decorations around flower gardens and such. And then there's the box of horseshoes, those handmade nails, and the tools we found too. Did you notice the hand pounding on the iron? And that fine saw with the engraving on the wooden handle? Did you see that? Men, that's a collectors' find and Matthew can keep or sell that stuff, and I bet we find more with the magnets."

Leo's oldest son, Johnny, pulled a large folded snaffle bit from his pocket. "Sir, I picked this up in the barn, too."

It was a workhorse bit and Matthew took it in wonder. Just thinking of his great grandfather's big hands unbridling his horses and hanging their gear in the old barn silenced the big man for a moment. Another memory. This seemed to be the day when the past pushed into the present and Matthew was set somewhat off balance by all these thoughts.

Ralph said more about magnets and Matthew came back from the past and began his argument again. Their friends watched the exchange with amusement. Between Matthew's stubborn Danish roots and Ralph's equally stubborn German ones, it looked to be a standstill. Matthew protested one more time, but his big voice was silenced by the solidarity the men projected concerning this work they had started.

Fred grinned and stuck his chin out and Matthew understood Fred's jutted chin. He had run into it before. It was a long, strong chin, just like the rest of Fred. No one ever got to do things their own way when Fred's chin was set, and this time it was set in Ralph's favor.

"Okay, guys. You win. Ha! I guess I win, that is." He nodded and turned away to pick up a few very old handmade bricks lying around the area. Carefully he put them in his pickup. He knew Bonny would be tickled to use them in making a new flowerbed. It seemed right to handle something that his great grandfather had actually worked with. *I gotta come back and get them all* he thought, but now he wanted to show his wife their beauty. Maybe he'd use them to make a permanent flower box on the porch, or a couple of big square ones on each side of the walk. She'd like that too.

It gave Matthew a feeling of connection to the old gentleman, something he had never thought of and he suddenly thought of visiting the graveyard up behind the church. He'd do it on the very next Saturday he took Bonny into town. It was long past time for him to clean the weeds around the Larsen section of the cemetery. *Bonny will like that* he thought and grinned to himself. He could already see her bustling about and preparing flowers to be planted around the family graves. Her side of the family was buried up there too. *Billy is buried there and a visit to the site would comfort her.*

Matthew stood with his big hands resting on the rough bricks in the bed of the truck as he soberly considered his son, the army, and the flag in the box on the fireplace mantel. He shook his head in remorse for not taking his wife to the graveyard, especially when she wanted to go tidy up there. She didn't grieve now as at the beginning for they were able to talk about their son, and they only became really sad once in a while, like around his birthday, or at Christmas. Their faith comforted them, telling them that Billy was not in the ground but in heaven along with all the grandparents and other relatives. For Matthew it was enough. He never felt a need to visit the cemetery.

Today however, on the old place where his great grandfather had labored and where his grandfather and father had been born, something was happening to him. Matthew was finding a connection, a realization of the direct succession from one generation to another. Although they no longer had a son on earth, or the hope of having natural grandchildren, still life continued.

Matthew turned over another handmade brick and studied its irregular features. It was one that his great grandfather had laid into the house's chimney. The big man then vowed never to neglect this part of his wife's wishes again. If graveyard visiting from time to time made her happier, then he'd take her and that was that.

Back at the home place, Blackie's kittens were the hit of the day. They were large now and scampered everywhere in the barn. The visiting children chased and played and petted, and then fell exhausted on the straw bales holding the kittens. Before the day was over, Blackie's fluffy kittens all had new homes and Blackie sat in the rafters with her nose down on her paws, a sad but happy feral cat. Her little family would not have to grow up like she did. She was pleased.

Pounce watched with interest to see which family would take the calico kitten. It was immediately loved and caught by the little granddaughter, Mandy Cree Lee, of the Chinese veterinary, Dr. Lee. It seemed a fitting home for the little mixed kitten to Pounce. He had heard bits and pieces of the story about Dr. Lee and his mixed family of Chinese and Native Americans and was eager to hear the entire tale.

"See," Catcher whispered to him. "I told you she was an ordinary kitten and she's going to an ordinary home too." Both cats laughed for joy and not in mockery. They knew, as some did not, that skin color, or in this case hair color, meant nothing, and that all creatures are the same underneath their skins.

The adult cats were also fussed over and petted into meltdown most of the day and the Yellow Boys had never received so much attention as they ran from one petting hand to another. Catcher was especially targeted. Her coat shone in the sunlight, and the children seemed captivated by her wide bands of swirling black and silver hair. The little ones ran their fingers down the swirls and followed the pattern all over her body. Catcher did a lot of rolling over in the straw for them. The sweet little petting and pawing hands seemed to make her day. She purred herself into total bliss.

The boys obeyed Matthew and gave rides to every child on the place; even the smallest child rode the famous horses that day. Of course a few mothers had to walk alongside to hold them on. The rhythmic footfalls of the steady horses made the children sway as they rode and many hooted and laughed with delight. Mothers rejoiced in seeing such pleasure on the faces of their children and, from that day forward, the small children looked at little Leo and Henry with awe. These were the boys who had handled the Morgan horses. This was a fact the two boys would use in the future.

For several hours Trump and Spade walked steadily around and around, only stopping and standing quietly by the wide edge of the horse trough by the barn while children piled on and off. They nickered back and forth, and had a great talk about this clean-up business, without really understanding that the buildings were being torn down. They were especially interested in the fields they would soon graze on at the old homestead. The cats continued to scurry up and down on the fences, begging to be petted by the children waiting in line and the cows refused to go to the river to graze because of the bull and the way the horses kept walking up and down carrying the laughing children. This entire business seemed very un-farm like and was puzzling to the cows, so they grazed close by to keep their eyes on the strange activity.

After all the children had ridden numerous times, the Svensen boys rode down to the noisy river where the horses splashed and drank the water. Never had the boys felt more grown-up than while sitting confidently on the beautiful Morgan horses and never had

Spade and Trump fell more pleasure than when delighting the children.

Wally had his paws full the entire morning as he went from one group of animals to another, trying to keep some degree of calmness among them. A little girl named Gudrun, but everyone called her Goody, walked with the dog. Gudrun, a Scandinavian name not easily pronounced except locally, was the only granddaughter of Leo Svensen. She had wanted a rough collie ever since the second grade when she read the book, *Lassie, Come Home.*

Gudrun was only seven, could read like an adult, had four older brothers, and melted everyone's heart that knew her. Her excitement about anything literary had many buzzing about what she might become as an adult. Now, however, it wasn't books or language that interested her; it was Wally. So she walked with her small hand buried in his ruff as he made his rounds.

Wally didn't know how she longed to have a rough collie, but he felt her affection for him and he returned it gladly. This small, blond girl was much like his boy Billy, but Billy had been older. Yet the dog felt memories surfacing as he licked her hands and face and started out on another swing around the farm.

Lady lay in her pigpen and watched with interest, but she was more interested in her almost grown piglets. She knew they would be taken away soon. She sighed and stuck her nose back down in the dust and rooted.

Finally after all the riding, the horses were turned loose and, with the cows, they began wondering off toward the river. The cats and children checked out the luncheon tables and hurried out of the way of the women who waved aprons and spoons at them with, "Shoo cats! Shoo kids!"

So the children gathered on the warm straw bales leaning up against the barn and petted the cats into full meltdown as both groups waited for the men to return and lunch to be served. Wally plopped down on the straw near the barn door with Gudrun and in a few minutes both dog and child were asleep.

A few other sun-warmed cats and kids fell asleep in the yellow straw also, and only stirred when the trucks drove into the yard and the lunch gong sounded an hour later.

At the clanging of the porch gong, those working on the overgrown trail between the old pastures and the new pastures knew the men had returned, so they started walking back across the pasture. The college-age group from Peace Lutheran had set themselves to cleaning this trail and had done a good job, laughing through the morning hours especially when the boys found it necessary to tumble or push each other into the river. Yet by lunchtime they were mostly dry again.

An engagement of marriage came out of that segment of the work party. Betty Patterson accepted Gregory Lundquist's hand. On a wildly overgrown part of the trail when he was finally able to get her alone, he asked her to marry him. Gregory had been trying to get her alone a few minutes from the group for weeks so that he might ask her this important question. He worked nights and she worked days, and it had been difficult to even ask her out on a date. So, he finally decided to simply ask her to marry him, and plan on dating her after the wedding.

The two young people knew each other well but had never dated, a fact Gregory laughingly told accompanied by blushes from his bride to be. Everyone laughed and enjoyed his joke, not realizing that it was true. Handshakes, hugs, and congratulations went around the yard after that. It was said by someone later that a work party should be held at least once a year making sure to invite the Danish bachelor brothers, the Andersen boys, and the Norwegian spinster sisters, also Andersons, but spelled differently. Of course, this was said in jest, and the men and women in question laughed along with the others as they all gathered at the luncheon tables, though several people thought they saw sideways glances between the folks in question.

Reverend Bergstrum offered a simple blessing before the entire party fell to the meal in front of them. "Father in heaven, thank you for this bounty and bless the ladies that prepared it. You have provided again and we are grateful. Amen."

Choruses of "Amen" echoed in the yard as the women served paper plates of food with small cups of juice for the small children on the porch first, where cleaning up after them would be as easy as picking up a broom. The rest of the folks sat wherever they could with a number of teenagers claiming straw bales in front of the barn and the older folks sitting down at the sawhorse and plywood tables on the lawn.

When the stomachs of all the diners were way too full, the men sat with their coffee and planned the next phase of work. Matthew scheduled his haying with the Andersen brothers and inwardly planned to go check the big hay shed in the east pasture by the highway before haying began. He wanted to make sure it was clean and ready for the new bales. The concrete floor he'd had laid in it several years previously had been a good investment. Since then, he'd not lost a single bale to mildew as the bales sat above the concrete on wooden pallets. It was easy for local buyers to back their trucks right up into the shed when they came to buy hay.

The men talked about returning to walk the fence lines and making any necessary repairs to the old homestead fences. Matthew protested, but the whole job seemed out of his hands now. He protested again and said he'd hire a man to check all the fences before winter. The men just grinned at him, ignored the farm owner, and kept right on planning the fence checking.

So Matthew gave up and walked down to Brawny's pen on the east of the barn and began scratching the head of his big Randall bull. His mind was full of conflicting feelings and his heart was swollen with emotion. Grown men showing love openly to other grown men was hard on this farmer. He was beside himself with thoughts. He wanted to pay them for their work, but knew the offer would offend. *Maybe he'd pay just the young men.* No, that would not be right either. He fussed with himself internally.

When his cougar-removing buddy, Fred, had said, "Let's clean up this old place," it had sounded good. Matthew hadn't realized that it would become such a big work party with so many neighbors. Fred seemed to have invited the entire county. Matthew was embarrassed. He wanted to accept the help graciously, but grace toward men wasn't in his character. Loud was how Matthew dealt with his feelings, and in this case, loud would not have moved his friends in the slightest.

Matthew bent his head closer to the slightly curled facial hair of his bull whose long black eyelashes blinked in pleasure at the scratching going on around his ears. The man grunted and fumed. *I'm perfectly able to care for my place.* Then he thought of why he sold his cows. *Milkin' that many had gotten harder, and I want to breed a few heritage cows. And why do I now hire the hayin' done too, instead of doin' it myself? I'm older, that's why.*

He sighed and admitted to himself that it had become too hard to maintain his equipment anymore. The work was too much for him now. And, he *was* getting money for hay instead of having it spoil on the ground. He'd also done well when he sold his big mower and baler. Matthew grunted in the bull's face and the bull blinked at him and went back to pulling hay and chewing without comprehension.

"Am I a gentleman farmer, bully boy? Others do my work and I get credit for it?" Matthew grunted again and pulled his bull's face hair even harder as he scratched. Brawny groaned in pleasure, "Huhh."

The cluster of men planning the fence-checking party watched Matthew standing in the bullpen with satisfaction. "Ha," Fred said as he laughed quietly. "We got the big guy this time. How many times has he helped us over the years? I don't remember us ever gittin' him to back down and let us help him. At least not on this scale."

"Yah. Dose big shoulders lifted my calves out'a da water, one by one, when we was flooded dat time," Leo Svensen nodded vigorously as he remembered how other neighbors had lost livestock but they had lost none. His son, Carl, dropped a warm hand on his dad's shoulder as they stood remembering the year of the bad flood. Then he told the story about trying to lead bawling cows out of a flooded field.

"It was like this. The cows would not leave their small spring calves and Dad's size and age would not permit him to carry a calf anymore. So I lifted calves as Dad attempted to lead cows without a lot of success. Those dumb cows just milled around on the only knoll in that pasture and didn't get the point that they would have to go into the water to get to the shallow end and then up on dry ground again."

Carl grinned and the men laughed but Leo just stood quietly and listened to his son.

"Matthew and Bonny arrived with Wally just then and Matthew waded into the river water along with me and we crossed to the knoll and began carrying calves back on our shoulders while the mama cows followed. Then Dad and Bonny hustled the rescued animals up the hill into the barn with the help of our dogs and Wally. All the while the water in the field was rising and on the last two trips, the water had risen from Matthew's waist to his chest."

"To his chest? Man, that's bigger than me." Ralph knew the story but had never heard about how fast the water had risen during the calf rescue.

"Ralph, everything is bigger than you," Fred shot back while the men laughed.

When the laugher subsided, Carl went on. "I'm not tall enough with a calf on my shoulders too, but Matthew went right back and got the last couple of calves with the cows swimming a short distance behind him. Ha! Seeing their calves in front of them across the big man's back caused them to follow him through the water until they were reunited. They would have followed him through fire, I think."

The guys laughed again and Carl squeezed his father's shoulder. Then several other men told their stories of when Matthew had been there for them. The bond grew stronger as they looked across the yard to where Matthew stood with his bull. They knew why he struggled, just as each of them had at one time or another. Somehow standing with their animals seemed to help them all.

Several men from town stood and listened to the stories of these farmers. They didn't have to rescue calves during floods, or trap cougars, or even mend fences. Their lives were quite different. Still some of them had also benefited from Matthew's kindness during difficult times over the years and they nodded with understanding that all men need to accept help at some time or other. One of them, Ronny Davis, a young man who worked evenings for Ralph at the hardware store, offered his take on Matthew by suggesting that maybe standing with a bull was not a safe place to be. That broke the moment and the men laughed again, and even the country men agreed that bulls should never be completely trusted, but said that this one was still pretty young and Matthew was an old hand at raising and handling bulls, especially as they become mature ones.

In the bullpen the bull's low "Huhh" settled Matthew and he straightened up, at least on the inside. If his friends and neighbors were going to help him, then so be it. He would say thank you and not argue, or offend them by offering to pay them. That afternoon, Matthew swallowed more than saliva and dust in the bullpen. He swallowed his pride. When he left Brawny to return to the men, he was still Matthew, a good man, but now a much humbler one.

Pounce and Catcher lay under a luncheon table while the men talked and listened to the stories they told. All this had happened before Catcher came to the Larsens and she was fascinated at the thought of a calf across Matthew's shoulders. The only young she had ever seen carried was when mama cats in her first home carried their kittens. As usual, Pounce listened carefully but just didn't get the picture for he was a very visual cat, and most of the time, needed to see things to understand them.

Peace Lutheran's young people finished lunch and wandered back down the trail along the river, but now they just walked the part of the trail they had opened up while they planned their next work party.

Betty Patterson and Gregory Lundquist walked a little apart from the others, holding hands, and the ladies and teenage girls cleaning up the luncheon all stopped to watch and sigh as the couple left for the river. Romance did not die in the farmwomen just because there was much work to do or because many of them were getting older. Romance lived on in the difficulties of farming, and in what they shared with their husbands, and in the careful raising of their children, and was especially celebrated in every new couple among them that found each other.

Dr. Lee spoke quietly to Matthew about his coming back to check the livestock later in the fall. "Now Matthew, when I return, I don't want Bonny telling me about anymore sewing up of animals around here. That's my job and you must know it's too painful for the little creatures without me dulling the area you're sewing on."

"Yah, yah. I promised Bonny not to have her sew anything up anymore, but it was just cats and ..."

"Matt, you'd call me in a flash if it was one of your horses or a cow."

"Yah, but ..."

"No sir. Won't do. Go with your wife on this one. No more doctoring of cats or other animals with old meds and nothing to dull the pain. And what about infection? That's the real rub. You've been lucky. Catcher was hurt, yes, but that Pounce cat was seriously injured."

"Yah, okay, Doc. You want a side of pork this fall, or money again? I hear Chinamen like pork."

Both men laughed and the big one slapped the short one's back while the short one slapped somewhere just above the big man's waist.

"We'll see, my friend. We'll see."

Small children were sleeping everywhere. It seemed every straw pile had a child in it, and seven of them were clutching sleeping, half-grown kittens. By now, the cows and horses were grazing down by the river and the cats were curled here and there in the barn, also fast asleep.

The only noise was the bawling of the half-grown calves wanting to be put out in the pasture with their mothers, but Matthew didn't want the job of separating them later when he milked. So he just gave the calves extra hay and a bit of grain and they settled down to steady munching.

The women were tired too, but like countrywomen everywhere, they divided the leftover food among them, and kept washing and talking and packing until everything was neat and clean again. Finally, the men put the extra sawhorses and sheets of plywood used for tables back in the storage area of the barn, loaded their cars and trucks, and declared it was time to go home.

It was only three o'clock in the afternoon, but all the farmers still had their chores to do and some had a number of miles to drive before reaching their homes. Reverend Bergstrum called to all, "Come on now. Let's have a prayer before we go," and the company bowed their heads where they stood.

"Our heavenly Father, we thank you for the kindness you have shown us today for we have found joy in work and strength in helping others. These good people have assisted their neighbors, and we pray that you will richly bless them for giving their gifts to their friends. Now, our God, we thank you for the gift of eternal life through our faith in Christ, who is the best gift of all, and we also ask you to bless our community. Help us to live among our neighbors in a way that honors Christ who walked among us so long ago, and who still walks among us today in your people. In Jesus' name, amen."

Several non-churchgoers were moved by the prayer, but wondered at the possibility of that last request. Even Gregory Lundquist, of the college-age youth group, wondered. *Does God bless whole communities? Everyone?* He hadn't heard his pastor pray like that before, or at least not that he could remember, and this idea caught his fancy. Gregory's mind raced as he resolved to speak to Reverend Bergstrum about whether God really would bless sinners while he blessed saints, for he was a religiously minded young man and took every word at face value. It had never occurred to him that God might bless a lot of people at the same time, even some who were not considered godly.

So, while others were beginning their good-byes to one another, Gregory stood and planned his argument against a general blessing coming on all men. Just then, a bit of stray scripture floated into his mind ... *be the children of your Father, which is in heaven ... He sendeth rain on the just and on the unjust ...* Gregory was jolted and hurried around the group of friends to speak to Betty. He wanted to tell his bride-to-be that for the first time in his life, he thought he had heard from God. Much as the cats forgot their resolutions, Gregory forgot his against God's general blessings as he dashed to find her.

Most of the work-party friends felt that something warm and living had been transmitted between them as they shook hands and hugged all around. It was sobering, for many of them realized that they had both given and received a very special kind of friendship, one based on really getting to know others by lifting the spirits and the loads of one's neighbors.

Pounce slept in the barn that night and Bonny was tired and didn't think of him. All of the farm cats tumbled into the loose straw, and stirred only to stretch out and feel the touch of one of their sleeping friends. This was especially comforting to Blackie, since she wasn't curled up with her kittens anymore.

By early morning, in the coolest part of the day, a mound of black and white, two shades of grey, and several shades of pale yellow lay all jumbled up nicely together. Tails and noses and paws were stuck here and there, and it was hard to see where one cat began and another ended. Their warm and cuddled friendship made a lovely picture painted in cat hair. Later, their furry coats were tipped in bright splotches of light when the early morning sun came streaking through the barn.

The painting was complete. The kitties appeared much like their human friends when touched by light, for when sharing with one another, they tended to become almost hopelessly tangled in the wonderful delight of living.

CHAPTER 14

Teachable Cat

The silo caper had gone to Pounce's head. He started trying to appear wise, and it was blotching up the good he had done. With his little black and white cathead filled with important thoughts about himself, he was beginning to try his friends' patience.

One evening he spoke to Catcher. "Dear, I'm trying out this new idea." He stood taller and tried to lower his voice. "What if I have a real talent to lead others and don't use it? Would I suffer? Would the farm suffer?"

Catcher listened, her green eyes growing dark and narrow. Finally she spoke, but it wasn't what Pounce wanted to hear. "Pounce, Wally led us and don't you forget it! You had the idea, the great idea of a team attack. But, it was Wally that led us. All of us!" She was peeved and Pounce could see and hear it.

"But, Catcher ..."

"No, Pounce. No buts. Why don't we hear Brawny and Lady bragging about holding the door closed on the silo? They were just inches away from the claws of that raging big cat. Instead, they sat down and kept her in there, protecting us all."

Pounce sat still, his eyes lowered and his whiskers drooping toward the floor.

"Or the cows. I don't hear them bawling about how they mooed so loud it kept the cougar confused. And what about the rest of us? We were on the roof of the silo with you too, you know."

"But, I only meant ..." His voice trailed off. He sighed heavily and flopped down on the barn floor. Catcher was chewing him out and it hurt. He could not deny the points she made. She was right. Pounce felt some confusion as he examined his own heart.

Catcher was not finished. "It's Wally we ought to thank. He took your tiny cathead idea and turned it into a master plan that worked." She paused, looked at her sad love and then continued in a softer voice. "Then remember how he thanked all of the animals? He honored you when we were on the silo roof, but he thanked *all* of us. Pounce, you must get it together. You are acting badly now."

Pounce felt the warmth return to Catcher's voice as he raised his head. "I've made a mess of things. I'm a mess. Forgive me?"

She saw the remorse in his eyes and heard the catch in his voice. "Of course I forgive you. You are not a mess, just a funny, city, pussycat with a short memory. Now, you need to talk to the other cats. Your behavior, these last couple of days, has hurt them."

"Yup. Right on it." Pounce got up and went looking for the Yellow Boys and Blackie. They were high up on the straw bales in the back of the barn and Pounce sat down on the floor and looked up. "Hi guys."

"Hey, city cat," Big Yellow called flatly. It was unlike him to speak without emotion or drama, but Pounce understood.

Blackie looked down and said nothing. Little Yellow looked, and then turned around and lay down.

"Look, gang. I came to ask you something and to tell you something."

"Yeah. Like what?" Big Yellow retorted.

"Like, can you forgive a hard-headed, ignorant house cat who has never had cat friends before, and doesn't want to lose the good ones he's got just because he's such a jerk and got the bighead over what everyone did, as though ... oomph!"

Big Yellow had leaped down on Pounce followed by Little Yellow. The three boy cats went after each other with great delight, nipping, yowling, and tumbling around on the barn floor. The Yellow Boys savored every nip they got into Pounce's hide as he rolled and yowled and laughed and nipped them back. It looked like, but was not, a real catfight. It was instead the release of several days of tension between them. And it felt so good.

It was good also to Blackie as she watched and to Catcher, who had walked up in time to hear the entire Pounce speech. Some cat hair flew around as claws raked into hides without anger, so little real damage was done. The yowling was loud, and the slamming of cat bodies against each other, solid. It was cat brotherhood, a guy thing. And it was rough.

"Hey! Are all city house cats as ugly as you?" Big Yellow shouted as he held Pounce down while Little Yellow nipped into Pounce's hind legs and tail.

"Nope!" Pounce shouted back. "I'm the ugliest."

"Hey, cat, are all city housecats as dumb as you?"

"Nope again," Pounce answered, this time as he held down Big Yellow while Little Yellow, in the excitment of the chase, started chewing on Big Yellow's legs and tail. "I'm the dumbest!"

"That's what we thought," the Yellow Boys chorused as the three cats began to chase each other up and down the sides of the stall doors and across the bales of straw and hay.

The yowling and nipping continued throughout the barn as Catcher hopped up and sat down with Blackie on a bale.

"He'll do," Blackie began, "that guy of yours."

"Yeah," Her companion answered. Her eyes shone minty green. "He'll do just fine."

When all was quiet again and the boys were sprawled in exhaustion, Catcher called down to Pounce. "Now might be a good time to tell our friends how you feel about mice."

He sighed, sat up and decided that she was right, though he wished she had let him pick the time instead of announcing it. He sighed again and mumbled to himself. *It must be a female trait, this explaining of everything. Guys would wait and let their actions explain stuff, but females? No, they always talk about it.* Catcher could hear the mumbling but not make out the words. Pounce sighed the third time, and then let his love for Catcher take over. *If it was important to her that he explain how he felt, then he would.*

"Look, gang. This is the way it is. I love the hunt and I can sniff the little varmints out right away. I enjoy playing with them, and batting them high into the air too, just like you do. But putting them down, you know, finishing them off? I don't like that part. It makes me feel bad."

Pounce paused and sat quietly while the other cats watched him intently. "It's like this. When I was a kitten, I was owned by a sweet, but very old woman. Her grandson had a pet too." He gulped and shook his head, not really wanting to finish the sentence. "He had a little white mouse. He carried it around in his pocket."

Big Yellow stared at him and frowned and said, "What? A mouse-ski in the house-ski?" Both yellow cats began to laugh and hoot, and roll back and forth on the straw. They looked again at Pounce, and then laughed and rolled some more. When they saw his face still looking troubled, they tried not to laugh again. "Is there more?" They grinned impishly at each other and waited.

"And, and just recently," now Pounce did more than sigh. He lowered his head and groaned. "I caught a mouse in the chicken's cracked-corn barrel and, and I took it out to the field and, and I let it go."

Pounce heard the cats pull air into their lungs and saw the Yellow Boys and Blackie staring wide-eyed at him, so he went on talking, hardly knowing what to say. His words tumbled out and they were all mixed up with his emotional state. He began to stutter.

THE SONG OF POUNCE ➤

"I, I, I know it was wrong, but at the moment all I could think about was the, the boy, and the old lady, and, and the pet white mouse. Ah, you know, you know, ah, in the house with all of us, you know. I learned to play with it and not hurt it because if I did, I was slapped, you know, and I was just a kitten, you know. Finally, I learned that I wasn't to play with it like the toys they gave me, because those I could chew up. I had a favorite toy with a squeaker in it, and if I got rough with the live mouse, they gave me my toy to chew on and, and I learned. I learned ..."

Pounce's voice drained away. He sat in front of his friends and looked quite unraveled. Even his hair lay every which way. The other cats were a bit unraveled because of what he told them as well. But no one laughed anymore.

Then Big Yellow, looking at his friend, stood up. Somehow his normal scruffiness was not as noticeable as he stood in front of his companions, flat-pawed and erect. His tail was straight up and his ears open and high. Catcher knew that he was exercising leadership, even in his posture. It made her wonder if her attempts to educate him had helped. Regardless of the reason, his posture made her ready to listen.

"Cats. We have got us a problem. The way I seeze it, Pounce ain't afraid to kill mice. He's just fighting his early education. Now, we could reeducate him to our farm way of doing things, or we could help him fit in with the way he is.

"My take on this is that we have to do a bit of both. Ain't right somehow, a cat in the barn that don't hunt. On the other hand, ain't right somehow that we say everything he ever learned is wrong. Maybe in the city, they keep mice in their houses. That ain't right to my way of thinking. But city folks, they're funny things. Look what they did to Catcher. When she had a flaw, out she went. Nope, city folks are funny."

At this Catcher shook her head, not because Big Yellow mentioned her, but because it bothered her when he insisted on saying *ain't* instead of *is not* or *isn't*. She shook her head again.

"See how it troubles her? Even now?" He spoke compassionately, but Catcher sent cat daggers from her eyes toward Big Yellow. He tried to regain the high ground in his speechifying, but it had become sand under him and slid away. Big Yellow sank down and lowered his eyes. He was confused. He didn't get it. *Why did she look at me like that?*

Then the show cat relented and smiled at him. *He was thinking of my feelings after all. The Yellow Boys need understanding besides educating. They both have good, big hearts, just little brains.* Her own little brain had wondered far from the topic at hand. *Do cat brains grow inside their heads when information is put in? Maybe? I'll help the Yellow Boys.*

With that decision, she turned her attention back to the conversation. As she did, she completely forgot her resolve to help the Yellow Boys. She was brilliant for a cat, and loved to learn new things, yet it was also hard for her to focus on more than one thing at a time. Catcher was, after all, a typical cat in her thinking and cats seldom mentally multi-task.

Big Yellow stood up straight again, reassured by Catcher's smile as Blackie picked up the theme in her low gravelly voice. "Hey, he's our friend today and ain't no one's gonna be taking him away. Hey, the kid. He got a good mind, and he talked to the Wally collie dog just fine. Hey, any animal done give a plan to the dog, a plan, he said, for the silo beasts? Say, hey, we can't be a-forgetting him. Let him sniff out the critters, un-nerve and un-thatch 'um. And hey, we'll be right there to toss 'um on up and dispatch 'um."

Just saying the word "dispatch" made Blackie stop and lick her lips as her eyes glossed over, for she loved eating mice, especially the small, tender ones. "Hey! Hey," she finished up softly with her eyes closed, still licking her lips.

Pounce was sitting up straight by this time, all of his embarrassment gone, and he was itching to talk. "That's, that's why, why, why I thought I could sniff them out. But, I didn't realize that I appeared proud and I'm sorry and I shouldn't have thought that I was so brave by myself and ..."

"Pounce!" the cats shouted. "Enough!"

"Don't undo all the good bites we just put into that spotted hide of yours or we'll have to do it again," added Big Yellow.

"Oh. Yes. I see. So, maybe I could help sniff out mice, and you all could, well, you know, do it, ah, like Blackie said? Besides," he continued with a shy grin, "I don't like the taste of mouse. I like cooked food."

At this, his friends laughed. Blackie jumped down in front of him and touched his nose. "Cat, youse's a person, you know? What youse did here now ... you're alright, kid."

The warm emotion that everyone felt in the barn demanded action, and the Yellow Boys responded by singing. Pounce looked at them with delight. He didn't know they had song in them. Cat soul poetry poured out of those pale yellow faces and their whiskers twitched along while their tails kept the time.

"My fur is white and yellow
And I'm just another fellow
In the barn and on the farm.
There's mouse-ski in my tummy
And I find the mouse-ski yummy
In the barn and on the farm.
No matter what I think or what I fear
I know the reason why for I am here.
Oh, I'll let the cat-ski sniff 'em
And maybe Pounce will flip 'em
But then they're in my tummy
Yummy, yummy, yummy
All mine!"

By this time all the cats were singing and standing around the Yellow Boys. Matthew and Bonny were sitting on the porch that evening and enjoying the sunset when the cats started yowling in the barn. They listened; Bonny giggled, and Matthew chuckled. "Just what I need. Your Pounce cat has taught them all to sing."

The crickets, and other insects began joining in the chorus as the cows started softly mooing in the background. Once in a while the horses snorted at just the right time and Wally, by Matthew's feet, lifted his voice to give a few soft yelps in time with the evening concert.

By the time the full moon lit the sky, everything was quiet and peaceful on the Larsen farm. All the animals were settled and asleep in the barn or in their pens, and Matthew and Bonny where quietly snoring together in the house. Matthew slept and dreamed of a beautiful farm filled with peaceful critters and the love of his life quietly resting beside him.

Pounce and Catcher remained with the cats down at the barn that night. They sat on the hay bales outside the barn, long after the rest of the animals were asleep. Only Blackie and the Yellow Boys kept watch over grain bins deep within the cavern of the barn.

Outside, the two love cats talked and talked. Words of genuine friendship and respect, the root of all true love, played over and over again in their conversation. Moonlight, silhouetting the cats against the side of the barn, cast beautiful blue shadows over everything. A great artist could not have arranged their portrait in the moonlight more beautifully. Love and friendship always make a beautiful picture that's hard to duplicate. Maybe that's because an artist can only hope to capture an image without participating in the sorrows and joys of the image's life.

CHAPTER 15

Welcome Home

"Ah, girl. How many pickles I gotta eat come winter?" Summer was almost over on the Larsen farm and soon it would be time to go to the county fair. Bonny was pickling everything in sight it seemed, and Matthew walked around muttering about it. Bonny laughed but kept on making her pickles. She hoped to once again take a ribbon for her pickled vegetables. And the local farmer's market would sell all that she didn't keep. Bonny was well known in the community for her wonderful assortment of vegetable pickles.

Pounce was spending more time hunting these days, and Matthew noticed it and was pleased. Of course he didn't know that the cat was only sniffing them out for the other cats and still had no interest in actually killing one. The chase was fun, and flipping the little critters in the air was fun, but the ending was not. So Pounce continued to leave the dirty work to the other cats.

"You know, Pounce, one of these days Matthew will notice that you aren't killing mice. Everyone on a farm does his share of work. Cats hunt mice. What are you going to do?"

"I don't know, Catcher. The last mouse I caught looked me right in the eye just as I was about to finish him off. I'm trying, but just can't do it yet. But Bonny doesn't know how I feel yet. She still plays pounce the mouse with me."

"Pounce the mouse?" Catcher giggled. "You're a cat, not a mouse!"

"Yes, yes, but this is the game Bonny and I played while I was healing up in the house. It goes like this. I paw her and she pretends to chase me, and then I run back and paw her leg again. We just keep doing it until she falls laughing and panting in her chair. Then I get up on her lap and purr and it's so fine ..."

His voice trailed off and Catcher could see that he was reliving his house time with Bonny.

"Well, how does it go? Can I play too?"

"Sure. It goes like this.

"Pounce me and I'll pounce you
And we'll play pounce the mouse.
Meow! Meow! Let's have some fun
Pouncing through the house.
I'll tag you with a furry paw.
You tag me with your hand.
I'll chase you ... you chase me back
Pounce is where we land."

By this time both cats were chasing each other back and forth. They yowled and laughed, tagging each other over and over again. Blackie came down from her rafter perch and joined in. The Yellow Boys flashed to the noisy scene from somewhere, and were instantly in the middle of things, pawing and yowling as well.

"Cats!" Matthew bellowed at them, "What cha doin'?" The game stopped and the cats cowered in the barn aisle except Blackie. She was in the rafters in a second. Pounce knew what to do though. He walked right up to Matthew and rubbed his body against the man's leg. "Purr-ounce. Purr-ounce," he said loudly. Catcher took his cue and rolled over on the straw and pawed the air with her front legs. She looked beautifully appealing as she studied Matthew's face upside down.

"I got it! Just a cat game, huh?" Matthew chuckled that meltdown chuckle that they all loved so well. It had the sound of a warm rub about it, and it showed the soft underbelly side of the loud, strong man. It made the animals sense that he understood them and that he liked them. This time the big man didn't go from chore to chore like he usually did. He studied the cats, and then sat down heavily on the nearest straw bale.

"Come 'er, Catcher." She dutifully got up and walked over to him. After studying her green eyes carefully, he put his big hand under her chin and gave a gentle rub. Now she was on meltdown, but before she could fully collapse on the barn floor, he scooped her up and tucked her neatly under his arm. Rising in one motion, he ignored the other cats and headed for the door.

"Catcher?" Pounce called out in concern.

She turned her big green eyes toward him. He could see that she knew no more than he did. Pounce followed at a distance and stopped at the front door. It opened only to Matthew and Catcher and then shut in his face. He didn't know what to think. Part of him was glad Catcher had house privileges, even for a little while. Yet part of him was hurt that he was shut out. He was sure Bonny needed him too. *I'm sure of it*, he thought. He sat down in concern, and tried to think clearly, but good smells had escaped while the door was open. *It's almost evening and isn't that stew or gravy or something good I smell in there?* Pounce lay down on the doorstep like an old dog and waited.

Soon Wally came up from bringing in the cows and horses and seeing Pounce on the step, he woofed. "Hi, cat. What are you doing out here? No housecat life for you yet?"

It was a friendly dig and Pounce knew it, so he answered promptly. "Sir, Matthew came to the barn and picked up Catcher and took her inside and I don't know why."

"Oh, that. Well, you'll know soon enough, Pounce." With that said, Wally came up the porch and woofed. Bonny came and let him in and when she saw Pounce hesitating on the porch said,

"Come on, you Pounce cat. Family is family. You have to hear this."

The house was light and airy, and smelled of delicious things. The countertop and shelves were filled with pickled vegetables, canned vegetables, canned sausages, homemade rolls, and so many other delights.

Pounce couldn't see it all at once, but he did see that his dresser bed was closed, and his old food dish had been picked up. *I guess that's that,* he thought. *The barn is home to me now.* His mind was made up to have a good attitude, and so he did. Pounce turned to look for Catcher, and was surprised to see her standing on top of the little table between Matthew and Bonny's chairs. Matthew held her there and he was studying her carefully from every angle. "I'm not sure, Bonny. How do we know?"

"Because, you dear, foolish farmer, she's a show cat. That's how we know." Her voice was firm and confident as she looked from her husband to her cat with satisfaction. "This is a grand thing to do. You'll see."

Matthew just shook his shaggy head in almost the same fashion Wally shook his. It amused Wally who was sure Matthew had learned the trick from him. He lay on the rug by the door and grinned. Then he turned to look at Pounce who seemed frozen in one spot. Pounce had confusion written all over his face as he looked at Catcher and Matthew, and then over to Bonny and then back to Catcher.

Wally sat up. "Look, Pounce. This is the way it is. Catcher was a show cat before she came here. She's beautiful and papered. Do you know that that means?"

"N-N-No," Pounce answered slowly.

"It means that Bonny has it in her bonnet to take Catcher to a cat show and show her."

"Oh, no," Pounce moaned. "It would kill her. She hates the shows. This is so sad for her and, and, for me." He wailed a long sad wail "Mearrrough," before he noticed that the painful sound had escaped him. Bonny heard him and turned. Then she came over and picked him up. She sat in her own chair and cuddled him and petted him. He couldn't think and he didn't purr. He lay stiffly in her lap and looked at Catcher.

The show cat looked back at him with wide, anxious eyes from where she remained standing on the table, still held by Matthew.

"Look at them, Matthew. They don't know what's going on. Both babies are fearful."

"Bonny, they're our cats. They'll do what we want them to do."

The cats knew in their hearts that his words were true, but they wished for a moment they were not. Then the next few minutes changed their lives, and set in motion a series of events that no one could have foreseen.

Bonny continued to pet Pounce slowly. "Little Pounce, your girl friend will be alright. I promise. And you will always be with her."

Then leaning forward she gathered Catcher into her lap as Matthew handed the cat over. "Pretty Girl, I know you don't want to be a show cat, but this is just a country fair and this year, for the first time, there's a pet show for barn cats. You are the most beautiful barn cat anyone has ever seen. I'm sure you can win. Then when you and Pounce have your kittens, everyone will want them. We might even get to sell them. People take better care of what they have to pay for."

Bonny giggled and her lap shook the cats. "What do you think? It's how we can promise your kittens will find wonderful, loving homes. And," she said with finality in her voice, "they won't be show kittens since they'll only be half pure. Ha. Ha!"

That did it for Catcher, and she began to grin while she looked into Pounce's still puzzled face. "You silly city cat. Because you are, forgive me, an ordinary, mixed breed cat, our kittens will never go to the show ring like I had to."

With those words and understanding ringing in his ears, Pounce perked up. "You mean because I'm a," he cleared his throat, "a citified alley type cat, though house raised you understand ... but sort of a dud pedigree wise, our kittens will have a better chance at a normal life?"

"Yup, silly! Yup, yup, and yup!" Catcher giggled, using Pounce's usual way of responding.

"Well, pussycats. Will you do it for me?" Bonny hardly noticed the happy change to the cats in her lap who were now limp and purring. "I promise you, Catcher girl, you won't live in a cage or be taken away from Pounce and the farm. Not ever!" This last was said firmly. Bonny studied her charges as they nosed each other on her lap. "Well, what do you think, kitties?"

Matthew, by this time, was seated in his own chair and shaking his big head back and forth. *How pretty she is, even if she does talk to cats. Pretty, even after thirty-five years of marriage.*

Wally sat on the rug by the door, watched his master, grinned his collie grin, and shook his big shaggy mane back and forth also.

"Ah," Matthew exhaled loudly.

"What, dear? Did you say something?"

"Nothing. It's just good to sit a spell before milkin', though I know the ladies are waitin'. Right, Wall?"

"Woof." The big dog stood at the door, ready to go again.

"Look, Bonny. Old Wally is always ready. I pray God will help me to feel the same. This old body is creaking some."

"He does help, dear. He does." Bonny answered as she scratched the purring chins of her lap cats.

Matthew hauled himself out of his chair and joined the dog at the door. "Okay, big feller, cows and pigs and horses. Come on." Wally's head received several hard pats from Matthew's rough hand as they started out to finish the evening chores.

"Now, cats," Bonny continued, "Will you do it? Will we be a

family that tries out new things? Or will we be a family that is afraid of anything new because of the things we've suffered in our past?"

Pounce immediately thought of how the plan to take out the cougar had worked. *Why not Bonny's plan? Bonny wants it. We love Bonny. Her plan might just work.* Her assurance that they could remain together helped the cats relax. Now Bonny was inviting them into another adventure. This adventure would not have raccoons in the yard, or bulls with tubs tied to them, or kittens living in a hole, or cougars in a silo. Still, it sounded exciting, so they began to purr their approval.

"I knew it. You two want to try new things as much as I do. Okay, here's what we'll do. No more mouse hunting for you, Catcher. I don't want your coat torn, or damaged by sticker bushes. You will live in the house with me, and I'll learn to make your coat gleam like when you were cleaned up in the old days.

"Pounce, you will stay here and keep her company. You'll both be less likely to wander if you're together. Now, we've got to get a little cage for a carrier."

Catcher winced when Bonny mentioned the cage but Pounce licked her ears. "Catcher, it will be fine. Maybe Bonny will let me go in the cage with you. I'll ask real nice like, when it gets near time to go. Okay?"

Catcher nodded and relaxed again. The rest of the evening was quiet and uneventful. Little bowls of stew for the cats and a big one for Wally were set on the floor. The stew was delicious. Then Bonny bedded the cats down in the dresser drawer high up off the floor. She kissed their furry faces quietly when Matthew wasn't looking and whispered,

"Welcome home, Pounce. Welcome home, Catcher."

Maybe they would not get to live inside all the time, and that was fine because Pounce was beginning to think that being an inside and outside cat was more fun. Now, the only thing left to do was to explain to the animals why they had been taken to live in the house.

Pounce tapped his front foot on the edge of the dresser when thinking about it, and Catcher answered as though she had heard his thought. "Blackie will understand everything. The Yellow Boys will say, 'Huh,' and then go back to their wrestling and mouse catching. The chickens? They don't know anything anyway, except when the mice take their grain and Bonny takes their eggs. That's when we hear them squawking."

Both cats laughed out loud at the thought of hens making any sense by their squawking. Neither of them had ever learned to understand the chicken language. It seemed to them to be merely a response to things like laying an egg or warning of a weasel. Chicken squawks didn't seem to have thought behind them, or so the cats reasoned.

Catcher continued to speak as Pounce raised himself up and showed interest. "Lady is already sad because her piglets are mostly grown now and they go away at this time every year. But I understand that Matthew plans on keeping a couple of them until cold weather. So she will be cheered up no matter what we do. The cows will nod and chew their cuds in our faces when we tell them, but they won't really understand about a cat show. It's like you said ..."

Pounce finished her sentence by *quoting* one of his earlier songs.

"A cow has no poetry in her soul,
A cow has no poetry in her soul,
No matter what you say.
Her head is in her hay
For a cow has no poetry in her soul."

Pounce chuckled as he finished saying it, knowing the song wasn't true now, and he would not be singing it any more. After watching how brave the cows were in the cougar incident, he had learned that cows have a lot of music in their hearts. His mama had been right; every living animal does reveal its song not only by what it says but also by what it does.

"Catcher. This is a good lesson for me."

"What lesson?"

"It's only our minds that differ. We think different thoughts but on the inside we are the same. I need to sing a new song about cows; they do have poetry inside of them."

"That sounds wonderful."

"When we saw all the animals help to catch the cougar, it was great. My mama said that bravery is another kind of poetry, another kind of song, just like working together is."

"Really? That sounds like right, tight thinking." She giggled once more, this time at her own humor.

With her answer in his ears, Pounce rolled over on his back and hummed in thought. Catcher sat beside him and studied how white his whiskers were in comparison with how black his spots. With one paw she played with his whiskers while he hummed and finally broke into song.

"Randall Cattle once were chattel
Of beef and brawn and hides.
Helped to settle this country's mettle
And pulled its plows besides.
White back critters loved ma's fritters,
Big friendly creatures are they.
Randall cattle, do not saddle,
Let them eat their hay. Hey!
Let them eat their hay. Hey!"

By this time Catcher was on her back alongside Pounce, watching the waving of his little white feet in the air. She giggled to herself. *Would Matthew's cows come to Bonny's kitchen window to eat corn fritters out of her hand?* It actually wasn't too strange a thought for she'd often seen Bonny feed them a bit of grain out of her hands in the barn. Catcher snuggled in closer to Pounce and joined him in another round of the new song, her soft voice filling out the melody.

"Listen, Matthew, Pounce is singing again. Oh, and Catcher too it seems." Bonny dropped a loop of her wool yarn and had to pick it up again.

Matthew grunted as he examined yet another strap of leather, then slowly answered while trying to hide his grin. "Yah. Just what I need, two singin' cats in the house."

Both cats giggled as they finished their song and lay quietly. Then Catcher sat up and studied Pounce again. "Have you noticed how sweet the cows and Brawny are on each other these days? I didn't know cows could flirt. But some do, I guess."

"Cats flirt."

"I never did."

Pounce expression revealed that he was teasing again, so Catcher made a face at him and then continued. "Brawny will be glad there are two less cats sitting on his fence, so we won't be missed there. But we will have to explain to Trump and Spade why we are kept in the house. You know, when Bonny lets us out in the morning, we'll run down to the barn and tell them."

Pounce nodded and replied, "You said, you know. You know?"

Catcher nipped his ear. "You got it, huh? Good." She smiled at him, knowing he was teasing again.

"Yup. Got it." He nipped back. "We'll do it in the morning."

"I can hardly wait to tell them that we're going to the fair with them. I'd like to ride with them in the horse trailer if we can."

"You would?" Pounce was amazed at the thought and his eyes became wide as he looked at Catcher.

"Oh silly, not where we can be stepped on. I want to ride in that high part in front. You know, where the hay is piled for the horses to eat while they travel? Wouldn't that be fun?"

"Oh, yeah. The manger. Where we played and slept several times and where we crept away to be alone. Yeah, a good place." Pounce looked at Catcher. His eyes wrinkled up as tight as he could make them as he remembered and smiled a little cat smile. "The manger in the horse trailer, under the stars on a warm summer night with you. That is a great place."

Cats don't blush but Catcher, like most females, was touched when reminded of a romantic moment. She felt happy that Pounce had remembered where they had watched the stars. She knew it was not a male tendency to remember such things, especially among cats.

"Sweet Catcher," he whispered as he started drifting off, "good night."

She kissed his half open eye with her nose. "Good night."

"Oh, life is good, kitty," he murmured.

There they lay with their whiskered heads hanging out of the dresser as they sleepily watched Bonny work on another beautiful rug, finishing it up for the fair. Matthew also sat by the fireplace mending a piece of horse harness, and putting some kind of polish on the leather that made it gleam in the firelight. It was rich and chocolate brown, and oh, so shiny.

The final touch was when he used something to wipe the dull looking decorations. They became glimmering jewels on the brow bands of the horses' bridles. Matthew finished the bridles and reins and coiled them up carefully. Then he bent to the pile of leather on the floor at his feet and pulled out another piece of harness. Again he began checking every stitch and polishing every inch.

In their little cat hearts, the idea of attending the county fair was beginning to sound like exactly what Pounce and Catcher wanted to do next. Watching the careful, catlike attention Matthew and Bonny gave to every detail, they decided that fairs must be good, very cat-oriented events. At least they both hoped so. For now, both cats were in the house, and Matthew seemed to accept the fact. It was indeed a satisfying evening as Matthew bent over his harnesses and Bonny bent over her rug.

Firelight sparkled everywhere, bouncing its golden rays around the room. Sleepy, green eyes and drooping, yellow eyes followed the reflections. If the cats had not been so tired, they would have leaped after the rays as they flickered and danced across the walls. The logs continued to burn and light from the flickering fire painted the pussycats and everything in its path in moving specks of gold. That night, like the wool yarn Bonny wove into her rugs and the harness pieces Matthew polished and buckled to each other, everything on the Larsen farm seemed to fit together just right.

It was late, and the cats' paws and noses twitched almost in rhythm to the dancing light as they dreamed what pussycats dream about most: adventure, chicken gravy, running mice, and warm laps to sit on.

Pounce stirred and stretched. He yawned without fully waking and then slipped right back into his dream. His friends surrounded him, his belly was full, and his lovely Catcher softly snored beside him. Together they lay asleep in a tangle of toes and tails and furry elbows in their soft dresser drawer bed. Pounce was a very contented kitty.

End

A Few References

Reader, you may enjoy going online or to your local library to look up facts about your favorite animals in the Pounce story or to study more about country living. Maybe you live in a city or in an urban area and cannot raise livestock there. You can still have great fun learning how to plant container gardens and how to raise earthworms to help the soil.

Check out what you can do before you get discouraged about what you cannot do. Prepare yourself for a life of learning to enjoy, protect, and promote the wonderful animals and plants in our world. You will always need to eat so find out where your food comes from and how it is grown, harvested, shipped, and how it arrives on your dinner table. Here are a few places where you can learn more about some of the things mentioned in this story regarding the rural lifestyle.

Heritage Livestock Breeds: Information about American heritage livestock breeds is available by checking out the *American Livestock Breeds Conservancy,*
www.albc-usa.org.

"Like all biological systems, agriculture depends on genetic diversity to adapt and respond to an ever-changing environment. Rare breeds provide this genetic diversity along with essential attributes for survival and self-sufficiency. As agriculture changes, we need to be able to draw upon these breeds and their genetic diversity in order to serve future generations."

The marketing and communications manager wrote that statement to encourage your study of these valuable breeds. If you are interested in a variety of exciting and rare cattle and other rare livestock, you will love their website. Perhaps someday you will also work to help save an endangered and rare breed.

Randall Cattle: These are strong, landrace cattle and very likely the direct descendents of landrace cattle common in New England in the last century. The Randall Cattle Registry has the history of and lots of facts about this rare breed. They are highly intelligent, produce excellent milk and beef, and steers can be trained for oxen teams due to their calm dispositions.

Go to the Randall Cattle Registry online at http://www.randallcattleregistry.org and check out their official website for breed information and other related links. There you will see beautiful photos and read about the oldest farms helping to preserve these incredible cattle. The American Livestock Breeds Conservancy has placed this breed on their watch list because there are not many of them and the state of Vermont designated the Randall cattle as the State Heritage Breed of Vermont.

A special thank you to Phil Lang of *Howland Homestead Farm* who maintains the second oldest herd of Randall cattle. Phil provided the Pounce story with some interesting facts about these cattle. Visit his website and other Randall breeders to view these remarkable and beautiful cattle. You will love them too.

Morgan Horses: In America over two hundred years ago, Figure, a horse owned by Justin Morgan, became famous for his strength, endurance, gentle disposition, beauty, and for his ability to pass these characteristics on to his offspring. The Walt Disney Studios even made a movie for young people called *Justin Morgan*

Had A Horse to tell the story of Figure. He was the founder of the first American horse breed.

Morgan horses went on to influence other breeds including Tennessee Walking Horses, Quarter Horses, Standardbred Horses, and the American Saddlebreds. Morgan horses have been used as carriage horses, army mounts or police mounts, as ranch horses, workhorses, and for pleasure riding too. Many Morgan breeders also have web sites where you can view beautiful photos and learn more about this breed.

The American Morgan Horse Association sent me this statement for you. "The Morgan horse is known for many things: his extreme beauty and heart, his athleticism and versatility; his willingness and intellect. But his most important trait, the one that distinguishes him from all other breeds, is his people-loving attitude. The Morgan is a versatile horse within a versatile breed; he is the 'horse that chooses you.'"

You may learn more by e-mailing them at info@Morganhorse.com or by visiting www.Morganhorse.com.

Rough Collies: There are many online sites where you can research Collie dogs. Collie breeders, rescue organizations, kennel clubs, and other organizations dedicated to the beautiful "Lassie" type of collie dog are found across North America and in other countries. These original Scottish herding dogs were imported to the United States and have been working dogs, family companions, and show dogs ever since. Collies have changed over the years but good ones still maintain their beauty, loyalty, and desire to be the hard-working companion dogs they were originally intended to be.

Do your research at your local library and on-line and learn about the large Rough collies (like Lassie), the Smooth (a short-haired variety), the Border Collie, and other working dogs like Wally's friends living at the Larsen's neighboring farms.

American Shorthair Cats: Silver Classic Tabby cats are the most popular color of this cat breed. There are many websites featuring these cats. Go on-line and visit the breeders, read the cat magazines, and look for the history and the photos showing these beautiful cats. A good cat is still a valuable working animal in the control of rodents and purebred cats will hunt and catch as many mice as mixed breeds.

Other American Cats: Pounce, the hero of this story, and the companion cats in the author's home have all been adopted from local shelters. Animal shelters across the country are full of highly adoptable kittens and cats, both pure breeds and ordinary mixed breed cats. Some have been abused, others are there because their owners can no longer care for them, and many are there because their owners did not neuter them and they kept breeding.

Looking for a pet? Go online and check out what is available locally. Your next best friend may be waiting for you at your local animal shelter.

American SPCA: The American Society For the Prevention of Cruelty To Animals is an old organization. Today, the International SPCA helps save thousands of animals every year around the world. Young people and their parents can volunteer at the shelters and also become foster parents for dogs and cats. It's another way to become involved in animal care.

Animal Planet, the television show, runs the *Animal Cops: Houston* as well as other animal rescue television series from other cities. These are humane rescue shows featuring some of the men and women who work for or with the SPCA to rescue abused or neglected farm animals, pets, and wild animals. You can see the rescues in progress and learn many things about this type of work. Check your local television listings for these and other related shows to learn more about caring kindly for animals. Then go online and learn more about the SPCA.

The Humane Society of the United States: This society is deeply involved in animal rescue operations after major tornados, floods, and other natural disasters across the country. They are well equipped and trained to aid families who are uprooted by natural disasters. They also are involved in educating the public on all kinds of animal abuse, animal fighting, puppy mills, and other kinds of animal cruelty. Their web site has videos about their work with pets, livestock, and wild animals and puts human and animal faces on the stories we often read about in the news. They also use many trained volunteers to aid in these efforts. Check their website at http://www.humanesociety.org and see some video footage of their rescue work as it is happens.

Hobby Farms Publications: Some of my favorite reading is in the Hobby Farm magazines and websites. They have wonderful articles and terrific photographs of livestock, rural living, urban farming, and sustainability at www.hobbyfarms.com and at www.urbanfarmonline.com. These publications also feature special magazines dedicated to chickens, goats, cattle, etc., so no doubt they will have something special about your favorite farm animals. Also, check out their *All Farm Pets Farm Breeds* for a good look at many types of working farm dogs when you go online.

Farm Related Newspapers: Since I live in the northwest, I read **Capitol Press.** This is a weekly agriculture newspaper covering mostly Washington, Oregon, Idaho, and California. Their web site is www.capitolpress.com. Capitol Press gives crop reports, ranching and animal news, information about farming and ranching in North America, and even trade agreements with other countries regarding American exports of farm-related products. They also report on water rights and grazing issues, wild animals living near or on ranch land, plant diseases and organic farming, and many other kinds of farming.

Agriculture newspapers can be great learning publications.

NITA BERQUIST

You can learn about forestry practices too, and even about political issues in agriculture related topics. Look for such a newspaper in your area by going online or checking with your local library. Most feed stores and farm related stores have other publications about rural lifestyles as well.

Agriculture Colleges: Are you thinking of making farming or something related to it your life's work? Go online and check out the colleges and then talk to your school counselors, parents, and/or guardians. No doubt there is an agriculture college somewhere near you as North America has many of them.

National FFA Organization: This young people's society was also known as Future Famers Of America. Today, the organization recognizes that young people have varied interests concerning natural resources and it embraces those interests. The FFA helps young people develop life leadership skills in the careers of their choice, whether in food, fiber, or farming, and the science and business skills important to those choices.

This youth society is primarily for middle school and high school. Membership can begin as early as age twelve. They conduct career development events in many different areas including marketing, natural resources, business plans, etc., besides animal and agriculture events.

Check them out in your area by going online and see if a group like this fits with your goals.

4-H: This national youth society exists as a youth development organization. Millions of youth in America are members and active not only in rural areas but also in urban and suburban neighborhoods. They impact countless communities with over half a million volunteers and thousands of professionals working to assist young people to grow up and know they can make a difference in the world around them. The 4-H society is helping youth through hands-on training in a variety of fields such as animal and plant science, alternative energy, healthy living, etc. This organization is the youth's part of the United States Department of Agriculture cooperative extension service.

Visit their website at http://www.4-h.org and learn about their many programs and how you can receive regular 4H news and event information. You can also find the nearest 4-H office in your county online. This organization is open to young people from kindergarten through the twelfth grade.

Veterinary Medicine: Pounce and his companions go to a local clinic where they receive their annual shots and checkups. Pounce's veterinary is Doctor Davis and she told me why she became an animal doctor.

"Veterinary medicine is such a wonderful profession. We have the best of both worlds; we are able to heal animals and also form relationships with the humans who love them. Every day is filled with new adventures and opportunities to make a difference. I have loved animals since I was a girl. I spent all of my free time reading and learning about them. I also loved school, in particular, science. As I got older, I realized I could combine these two interests into a great career where I would be able to help both people and animals." ___Gina Davis, DVM, Covington, Washington

Those are really good reasons to chose a life's work with animals and people. Perhaps your love for animals will lead you to become a veterinary or cause you to enter some related field. Talk to your school counselors and teachers and ask them to help you select reading material and courses of study to help you pursue your dream. Go online and you will find many schools of veterinary medicine across the country.

Other Exciting Fields: Across the nation many programs are available to train you for a career concerning animals, food production, and a more natural lifestyle. The science surrounding these choices is endless, and you can indeed make a difference for both animals and people in such jobs as becoming a veterinarian assistant or as an expert in animal behavior.

Other related fields exist such as blacksmithing and the creation of special supplies and tools in relation to raising or working with animals. Think about handicapped riding organizations or animal rescue. Watch some of the television programs that feature trained individuals who remove dangerous wildlife from homes, educate hoarders to give up their suffering animals, or prosecute those involved in animal cruelty, etc.

Go and spend time in a pet store studying all the products there. Ask to visit a farm or ranch, feed store, tree farm, or plant nursery. Talk to professionals wherever you are and get ideas. Most people like to talk to young people and share their love for what they do.

The list of career opportunities is huge. Perhaps you will design new barns and buildings, or invent a new medical procedure useful in saving horses. You may be the one to develop a new career and open the door for many others to follow. Listen, you may only get to raise a box of worms to use in a few flowerpots right now, but tomorrow your ideas for preserving good soil and raising healthy crops for people and animals may sweep the globe.

A Final Note To Young Readers: Remember the Pounce cat. He accepted changes when they came because life is all about growing and changing. He sang to help him learn and that kept him happy and peaceful. He saw that life needs beauty and he found it in poetry and song, in the art of beautiful wool rugs, in the silver swirls of a tabby cat, in the spotted hides of cattle, and in the soul poetry of other living things.

Pounce boldly embraced the work that needed to be done and learned to work with others. He also discovered that life's journey is about making a difference in the lives of others, even if his personal goals at first were to live somewhere safe, to be comfortable, and to eat chicken gravy.

Yes, this is a fictional story and it's been written for you and in memory of the original Pounce cat. So I hope you enjoyed the story, but mostly I hope you enjoy the journey of growing up. Don't be in a hurry; just keep on studying and dreaming big dreams for yourself. Then when it's time, pounce on your choice of work by really loving what you choose to do. You have an important life ahead of you for you are a valuable person.

___Nita G. Berquist

CPSIA information can be obtained
at www.ICGtesting.com
Printed in the USA
BVHW041721291022
650515BV00001B/11